THE LACQUER SCREEN

A Judge Dee Mystery

by

ROBERT VAN GULIK

CHARLES SCRIBNER'S SONS
NEW YORK

The illustrations on pages iv-vii show
the four panels of the lacquer screen.

3 5 7 9 11 13 15 17 19 K/P 20 18 16 14 12 10 8 6 4 2

Printed in the United States of America
ISBN 0-684-17633-5

DRAMATIS PERSONAE

Note that in Chinese the surname—here printed in capitals—precedes the personal name

Main characters

DEE Jen-djieh — Magistrate of the district Peng-lai. In the present novel he is staying for a few days in Wei-ping, another district in Shantung Province

CHIAO Tai — one of his lieutenants, who accompanies him on the trip

Persons connected with 'The Case of the Lacquer Screen'

TENG Kan — magistrate of the district Wei-ping

Mrs TENG — née WOO, his wife, called Silver Lotus

PAN Yoo-te — his counsellor

Persons connected with 'The Case of the Credulous Merchant'

KO Chih-yuan — a wealthy silk merchant

Mrs KO — née HSIEH, his wife

PIEN Hoong — a soothsayer

Persons connected with 'The Case of the Faked Accounts'

LENG Chien — a banker

LENG Te — his younger brother, a painter

KUN-SHAN — a thief

Others

'The Corporal' (LIU Woo) — boss of the underworld of Wei-ping

'The Student' (HSIA Liang) — a young hoodlum

Carnation — a prostitute

SUMMER

WINTER

I

He remained standing just inside the door of his library, feeling utterly confused. His vision was blurred, he did not dare walk to his desk. Leaning his back against the door-jamb for support he closed his eyes and, slowly raising his hands to his head, pressed his temples. The splitting headache was now changing into a dull, throbbing pain. His ears ceased ringing. He now could hear in the distant backyard of his residence the familiar sounds of the servants, starting again upon their household tasks after the siesta. Soon his steward would come with the afternoon tea.

With a tremendous effort he took hold of himself. He noticed with relief that his eyes were getting better. He quickly raised his hands and scrutinized them intently. He did not see any bloodstains. He looked up, at his large writing-desk of massive blackwood. Its polished top mirrored the flowers in the green jade vase. They were wilting; he idly reflected that his wife would have to replace them, she always chose them herself from the garden. Suddenly there was an empty feeling in the pit of his stomach. He frantically stumbled into the room and succeeded in reaching his desk. Panting heavily he made his way round it, supporting himself on its smooth edge. Then he let himself down into his armchair.

He gripped the armrests, steadying himself against a new attack of dizziness. When it had passed he opened his eyes. He saw the high lacquer screen standing against the wall opposite. Quickly he averted his gaze, but the screen seemed to move round with his eyes. A violent shiver shook his

1

tall, spare frame. Instinctively he pulled his loose house-robe closer. Was this the end, was he becoming mad? Cold sweat pearled on his brow, he thought he was going to be sick. He bent his head and looked fixedly at the document his counsellor had placed on the desk, trying desperately to collect his thoughts.

Out of the corner of his eye he saw his steward enter, carrying the tea-tray. He wanted to answer his obsequious greetings, but his parched tongue was thick and swollen. When the elderly man, sedately dressed in a long grey robe and wearing a black skull-cap, respectfully handed him a cup of tea, the magistrate quickly took it in his trembling hand and tasted it. If he drank more, he would feel better. Why didn't the doddering old fool go away? What was he waiting for? He moved his lips to make an angry remark. Then he noticed the large envelope on the tray.

'This letter, Your Honour,' the old steward said, 'was brought just now by a visitor, a Mr Shen.'

He stared at the letter, not yet trusting himself to raise his shaking hand and take it. The address, written in a bold, official-looking handwriting, read: 'To Teng Kan, Magistrate of the District Wei-ping. Personal.' In the lower left corner was the large red seal of the Prefecture.

'Since it is marked personal,' the steward said in his dry, precise voice, 'I thought I'd better bring it to Your Honour directly.'

The magistrate took the envelope and reached mechanically for his bamboo paper knife. As one of the hundreds of district magistrates, he was but a small cog in the colossal administrative machinery of the mighty Chinese Tang Empire. And although in his own district of Wei-ping he was the highest government authority, he was only one of the dozen or so district magistrates under the Prefect in Pien-foo. The steward was right, a visitor carrying a personal letter from the Prefect must not be kept waiting. Thank Heaven, he could think straight again!

He slit the letter open. It contained a sheet of official note-paper, inscribed with only a few lines.

'Confidential. The bearer of the present, Dee Jen-djieh, magistrate of the district Peng-lai, having attended a conference in the Prefecture and now returning to his post, has been granted one week's leave to be spent in Wei-ping, strictly incognito. Extend to the said Dee all possible assistance.'

The Prefect.

Slowly Magistrate Teng folded the letter. His colleague from Peng-lai couldn't have arrived at a more awkward moment. And why did the fellow come incognito? Was there trouble brewing? The Prefect was known for his unconventional methods, he might well have sent this man Dee on a secret investigation. Should he put him off, saying he was ill? No, that would excite the suspicion of his household, for he had been perfectly well in the morning. He quickly gulped down the rest of the tea.

Now he felt better. He thought his voice sounded nearly normal when he addressed the steward:

'Pour out another cup, then give me my formal dress.'

The old man helped his master to don a long robe of brown brocade, and handed him a square cap of black gauze. The magistrate tied the sash round his waist. 'You can now bring Mr Shen,' he said. 'I'll receive him here in my library.'

As soon as the steward had left, Magistrate Teng walked over to the broad ebony bench reserved for receiving visitors. It stood against the side wall, under a scroll-painting of a landscape. He sat down on the left corner and verified that only half of the lacquer screen was visible from there. He went back to his desk. Thank Heaven that he could walk

3

steadily again. But would his mind remain clear? As he was standing there, lost in thought, the door opened and the steward came in. He handed his master a red visiting-card inscribed with two large characters giving the name Shen Mo. In the lower left corner was added in smaller writing Commission Agent.

A tall, broad-shouldered man with a flowing black beard and long side-whiskers came in and made a bow, his arms folded in the capacious sleeves of his faded blue gown. His well-worn black cap showed no insignia of rank. Magistrate Teng answered his bow, and spoke a few words of welcome. Then he motioned his guest to sit down on the bench, on the left of the low tea-table. He seated himself on the other side and gave the steward who stood hovering by the door a peremptory sign to leave them alone.

When the door had closed, the bearded man gave his host a keen glance from his quick, alert eyes. He spoke in a deep, pleasant voice:

'I have long been looking forward to meeting you, Teng. Even when I was still posted in the capital, I heard you praised everywhere as one of our great poets. And also, of course, as an exceptionally able administrator.'

Magistrate Teng bowed.

'You are too kind, Dee,' he said. 'Now and then I scribble a few verses, just to while away an hour of leisure. I had hardly dared to hope that a busy colleague, well known as a connoisseur of letters and, moreover, as a zealous detector of crimes, would deign to glance at my poor work.' He paused. The dizziness was coming back, he found it difficult to continue the usual courteous exchanges. He hesitated, then resumed: 'His Excellency the Prefect stated that you are here strictly incognito. Does that mean that your visit is connected with some criminal investigation? Excuse my abruptness, but . . .'

4

JUDGE DEE HAS TEA WITH MAGISTRATE TENG

Not at all!' Judge Dee said with an apologetic smile. 'I didn't know that the Prefect's letter of introduction was so tersely phrased. I do hope it didn't cause you undue worry! The fact is that I found my duties in Peng-lai quite strenuous —doubtless owing to my lack of experience. Peng-lai is my first post as district magistrate, you know. I was just thinking of taking a brief holiday, when I was summoned to the conference on coastal defence in the Prefecture. My district faces the Korean peninsula across the sea, and our Korean vassals are rather restive at present. The Prefect kept me busy from morning till night. A high official from the capital was present also . . . well, you know how it is when one has to be at the beck and call of those exalted persons! The conference lasted four days, and when I get back to Peng-lai I'll doubtless find plenty of arrears to make up. Therefore I applied for a short holiday, to be passed as a tourist here in your district, famous for its many historical sites and its scenic beauty—so exquisitely described in your poetry. That, and that only, is the reason why I asked to remain incognito, and why I call myself here Shen Mo, a commission agent.'

'I see,' his host said with a nod. He thought bitterly: 'On a holiday, forsooth! If the Prefect had said so in the letter, I could have put him off for a day or two.' Aloud he continued: 'It is indeed a relief to be able to dispense with all the pomp and circumstance incidental to our office for a while, and to go about freely as a simple citizen! But what about the persons of your suite?'

'As a matter of fact,' Judge Dee replied, 'I took only one of my lieutenants along with me, an able fellow called Chiao Tai.'

'Doesn't that encourage, ah . . . undue familiarity on the part of your subordinate?' Teng asked doubtfully.

'I must confess I never thought of that!' the judge replied

with an amused smile. 'Could you recommend a small but clean hostel where we can stay? And what are the most important monuments that one should see here?'

Teng took a sip from his teacup. Then he said:

'I am distressed that your desire for anonymity deprives me of the pleasure of having you stay with me here as my honoured guest. Since, however, you insist, I advise you to stay in the Hostel of the Flying Crane, which has an excellent reputation and which is, moreover, located not far from the tribunal here. As to the sights, I'll introduce you to my counsellor and general assistant Pan Yoo-te. He was born and bred here, and knows every square inch of this town. Allow me to take you to him, he has his office at the back of the chancery.'

Magistrate Teng rose. As Judge Dee followed his example, he saw that his host suddenly tottered on his feet. He steadied himself, gripping the armrest of the bench with both hands.

'Aren't you feeling well?' the judge asked anxiously.

'Nothing, a slight dizziness!' Teng said with a thin smile. 'I am a bit tired.' He looked testily at the steward, who had just come in. He bowed deeply before his master and said in a low voice:

'I apologize for disturbing Your Honour, but the chambermaid just reported to me that the Great Mistress has not yet made her appearance after the siesta, and that the door of her bedchamber is locked.'

'That's true, I forgot to tell you just now,' Magistrate Teng said. 'After the noon meal she received an urgent summons from her elder sister to go to her country house. Inform the servants.' As the steward hesitated, Teng asked, irritated: 'Well, what are you waiting for? Can't you see that I am busy?'

'I have to report also,' the old man mumbled with evident

7

embarrassment, 'that someone has broken the large vase in front of the bedroom. I——'

'Later!' Magistrate Teng cut him short. He conducted Judge Dee to the door.

While leading him across the garden that separated the magistrate's residence from the tribunal, Teng said suddenly:

'I sincerely hope that during your stay here you will not entirely withhold from me the advantage of your conversation, Dee. Please call on me at any time. I have a vexing problem I would like to discuss with you, some time. To the left here, please.'

They crossed the large main courtyard of the tribunal compound. In the building opposite Teng preceded the judge into a small but very neat office. The lean man who sat behind the desk piled with official documents and files jumped up when he saw his chief. He motioned a maidservant who was trying to efface herself in a corner to make herself scarce, then came limping forward and made a deep bow. Magistrate Teng said in a measured voice:

'This is Mr Shen, a . . . ah, commission agent, who brought a letter of introduction from the Prefect. He wishes to stay here a few days to visit the sights of our district. You'll give him all information he needs.' And, turning to Judge Dee: 'You'll kindly excuse me now, I must prepare myself for the afternoon session of the court.' He bowed and left.

Counsellor Pan bade the judge sit down in a large chair opposite his desk, and made the common polite inquiries. But he seemed preoccupied and nervous. Since Magistrate Teng also had seemed rather short with him, Judge Dee surmised that a particularly difficult case was pending in court. But when he asked the counsellor about it, Pan quickly replied:

'Oh no, we have only the usual routine matters to deal

with in the tribunal. Fortunately this is a rather quiet district!'

'I asked,' Judge Dee said, 'because during our conversation just now the magistrate hinted at some vexing problem he was confronted with.'

Pan lifted his grey eyebrows.

'Nothing I know of,' he said. The same maid came in again. 'Come back later!' he snapped, and she quickly disappeared. Then Pan continued to the judge with a contrite expression: 'Those stupid girls! It seems that someone broke a large antique vase standing in Mrs Teng's private quarters. My master valued that vase highly, it was an heirloom. None of the maids wants to admit she has done it, so the steward asked me to question them and find the culprit.'

'Has the magistrate no assistant besides you?' Judge Dee asked. 'As a rule a magistrate has three or four lieutenants on his personal staff, doesn't he? And he usually takes them along with him to every new post.'

'Yes, that's true. But my master didn't follow that custom. He is a man of rather retiring disposition, you know, a bit stand-offish, if I may say so. I myself belong to the permanent staff of the tribunal here.' He frowned, then went on: 'The magistrate must be greatly distressed about that vase! I thought he wasn't looking very well when he came in just now.'

'Does he suffer from some chronic disease?' the judge asked. 'I too noticed the pallor of his face.'

'Oh no,' the counsellor replied. 'He's never complained about his health, and he's even been exceptionally cheerful of late. A month or so ago he slipped in the courtyard and sprained his ankle, but that has completely healed. It's the summer heat that bothers him, I suppose. Now, let me see what places you ought to visit first, Mr Shen. There is . . .'

He set out on a long description of the sights of Wei-ping.

Judge Dee found him a cultured man, well read and with a deep interest in local history. It was with regret that he rose at last and said he had to leave because his travelling companion was waiting for him in a teahouse, on the corner behind the tribunal compound.

'In that case,' Pan said, 'I'll take you to the emergency exit at the back. That'll save you making a detour through the front gate of the tribunal.'

He took the judge back to the magistrate's residence; despite his clubfoot he walked with ease. They went through a long, dark, windowless corridor that seemed to run round the house. As Pan unlocked the small iron door at the end he said with a smile:

'In a way this exit is also a sight of our town! It was built more than seventy years ago as a secret entrance, when there was an armed rebellion here. As you know, at that time the governor, the famous——'

Judge Dee hastily cut him short by thanking him profusely. He stepped out into the quiet back street, and walked along in the direction Pan had indicated.

He found the teahouse where he had left Chiao Tai on the next corner. Although the siesta was only just over, the open terrace was already crowded. Most of the tables were occupied by well-dressed people, leisurely sipping tea and nibbling dried melon seeds. Judge Dee walked straight to a table where a husky man was sitting, clad in a simple brown robe and wearing a round black cap. He was engrossed in reading a book. When the judge pulled back the chair opposite, the man jumped up. Judge Dee himself was tall, but Chiao Tai topped him by nearly an inch. He had the thick neck, heavy wide shoulders and narrow waist of a professional boxer. His beardless, rather handsome face lit up as he said:

'You are back sooner than I thought, Magistrate!'

'Less of the "magistrate"!' Judge Dee warned him. 'Remember that we are here incognito!' He took the clothes bundle from the chair and put it on the floor. Sitting down, he clapped his hands and ordered the waiter to bring a new pot of tea.

A very thin, bony man who was sitting slumped in a chair all alone at a corner table not far from theirs, suddenly looked up. He had a haggard, repulsively ugly face. A thin, long scar ran from his chin to the empty socket of his right eye. It disfigured his lips, giving his mouth the expression of a continuous sneer. He put a long, spidery hand up to his cheek, trying to suppress a nervous twitch. Then he put his angular elbows on the table. Leaning forward, he tried to catch what the judge and his companion were saying. But the din of the conversation going on at the other tables drowned their voices. Disappointed, he then concentrated on observing the pair intently with his one, malevolent eye.

Chiao Tai looked round. When he saw the ugly man he quickly averted his gaze and said to the judge in an undertone:

'Do you see that fellow sitting alone at that corner table behind me? He looks like some loathsome insect that has just crawled out of its shell!'

Judge Dee looked and said:

'Yes, he doesn't look very prepossessing. Now, what are you reading there?'

'It's a guide-book of Wei-ping that the waiter lent me. It was an excellent idea to break our journey here!' Pushing the open book over to the judge, he continued: 'Look, it says here that in the Temple of the War God there's a set of life-size statues of a dozen of our famous ancient generals, done by a great sculptor of olden times. Then there is a magnificent hot spring that——'

'The magistrate's counsellor told me all about it just

now!' the judge interrupted him with a smile. 'We'll be quite busy here seeing the sights.' He sipped from his tea, then added: 'My colleague here, Teng, disappointed me a bit, you know. Since he is such a famous poet, I had imagined him as a jovial fellow and a brilliant *causeur*. But he seems a bit of an old stick, and rather a martinet. He looked ill and worried.'

'Well, what can you expect?' Chiao Tai asked. 'Didn't you tell me that he has only one wife? That's rather strange, for a man in his position!'

'You shouldn't call it strange,' Judge Dee said reprovingly. 'Magistrate Teng and his wife are an example of conjugal love. Although they have been married eight years and have no children, Teng has never taken secondary wives or concubines. Literary circles in the capital have nicknamed them the Eternal Lovers—not without envy, I presume. His wife, Silver Lotus, is also known for her poetical talent, and that common interest forms a strong bond.'

'She may be good at poetry,' Chiao Tai observed, 'but I still think her husband had better add two or three nice young girls to his bedroom furniture, just to get inspiration from, so to speak.'

Judge Dee had not heard him. His attention had been caught by the conversation going on at the table next to theirs. A fat man with a double chin was saying:

'I still maintain that our magistrate made a mistake during the session this morning. Why should he refuse to register old Ko's suicide?'

'Well,' a thin man with a foxy face who sat opposite him said, 'the body hasn't been found, you know! No body, no registration! That's the official mind for you!'

'It stands to reason there's no body!' the fat man said crossly. 'He jumped into the river, didn't he? And the current is uncommonly fast. Don't forget the amount of

12

slope it has, the hilly part of the city is quite high. I don't say anything against our magistrate, mind you, he is one of the best we have had these last years. I only say that, being an official who gets his pay on the dot every month, he doesn't know a thing about the financial worries of us business people. He doesn't realize that as long as the suicide hasn't been registered, Ko's banker can't wind up his business. Since old Ko had many affairs outstanding, that delay may mean big losses for the family.'

The other nodded sagely. Then he asked:

'Do you have any idea why Ko should have killed himself? No financial worries, I hope?'

'Certainly not!' the fat man said quickly. 'Sound business, that silk firm of his, the largest in the province, I'd say. He's had trouble with his health lately, though. That'll have been the cause. Do you remember that suicide last year of Wang, the tea dealer who always complained of headaches?'

Judge Dee lost interest. He poured out another cup of tea. Chiao Tai, who had been listening also, whispered:

'Remember that you are on a holiday, Magistrate! And all the dead bodies that may be drifting around here are the exclusive property of your colleague Teng!'

'You are quite right, Chiao Tai! Does that guide-book give a list of jewellers here? I must purchase a few trinkets for my wives back in Peng-lai, as souvenirs.'

'A list as long as my arm!' Chiao Tai replied. Hastily leafing through the book he showed the judge a page. Judge Dee nodded and said:

'That's good, I'll have plenty to choose from.' He got up and called the waiter. 'Let's go, I got the address of a good hostel, not far from here.'

The ugly man at the corner table waited till they had paid and gone down into the street. Then he quickly got up and sauntered over to the table they had just left. He casually picked up the guide-book and glanced at the page it lay open at. An evil glint came into his one eye. He threw the book down and hurriedly descended from the terrace. He saw the judge and Chiao Tai standing farther on, apparently inquiring the way from a street vendor.

II

The Hostel of the Flying Crane was located in a busy street that led up to one of the city's many hills. Its unpretentious, narrow gate was right next to the gaudy shopfront of a large winehouse.

However, the spacious hall belied the modest exterior. The fat manager who sat enthroned behind an impressive counter gave the two men a searching look. He pushed a thick register over to them and asked them to write their name, personal name, occupation, age, and native place.

' Are you afraid of robbers? ' Judge Dee asked, astonished, as he moistened the writing-brush. As a rule, one registered only one's name and occupation.

' Nothing of the sort! ' the manager said crossly. Pushing the book over to Chiao Tai he added importantly: ' My hostel has a high reputation, I can afford to pick my guests!'

' A pity your mother couldn't pick you! ' Chiao Tai said as he put their clothes bundle on the floor and took the brush. The judge had written ' Shen Mo, commission agent, 34, from Tai-yuan.' Chiao Tai scrawled next to it: ' Chou Ta, Mr Shen's assistant, 30, from the capital.'

Judge Dee paid three days in advance, and a neatly dressed waiter took them to a simply furnished but very clean room on the third courtyard, far from the noise of the street.

Chiao Tai pushed the outer door open. It gave directly onto the courtyard, paved with marble flagstones. He turned round and scowled at the teapot which the waiter had just placed on the table. He said to the judge:

' We just had tea. This yard here has a beautiful smooth pavement, what about a few rounds of stick-fencing to

15

stretch our legs? Then we might take a bath, and have dinner in a restaurant outside to sample the local specialities.'

'Excellent idea! The long ride from Pien-foo this morning has made me stiff.'

Both stripped down to their baggy trousers. Judge Dee parted his long beard into two strands, which he knotted together at the nape of his neck. They threw their caps on the table and walked out into the courtyard. Chiao Tai shouted at a groom who was standing about there to fetch two fencing sticks.

The judge was an excellent boxer and swordsman, but he had only recently taken up, under Chiao Tai's guidance, the art of stick-fencing. This was not considered a sport suitable for gentlemen, being popular only among highway robbers and vagabonds. But Judge Dee found it a good exercise and had become quite fond of it. Chiao Tai was expert at this art, for before entering Judge Dee's service he had been a highwayman, as attested by the numerous scars that covered his broad, deeply tanned chest and his long, muscular arms. One year before, when the judge was on his way to Peng-lai, his first post, Chiao Tai and his blood-brother Ma Joong had attacked him on a lonely road. But Judge Dee's forceful personality had so impressed the two men that they had then and there given up their violent profession, and became his devoted lieutenants. In the past year the judge had found this formidable pair very useful for arresting dangerous criminals and executing other difficult tasks. He gladly made allowance for the fact that they had not yet quite acquired the respectful attitude becoming to a magistrate's lieutenants; he rather enjoyed their frank and outspoken manner.

'I take it that the manager won't mind us fencing here,' Judge Dee said as he took up his stance.

'One peep out of him and I'll smash his head down into

his fat belly ! ' Chiao Tai shouted belligerently. ' Then he can squint at the world through his navel. Mind your backhand swing now ! ' He went for the judge with a quick blow at his head.

Judge Dee ducked and aimed a long sweeping blow close along the floor at Chiao Tai's ankles. But Chiao Tai jumped over the stick with a supple grace surprising in so heavy a man, and followed up with a swift thrust at Judge Dee's breast which the latter skilfully parried.

For a long time one heard only the clattering of the sticks and the panting of the fencers. Soon a few grooms and waiters gathered in the yard, watching the fight. Intent on this free entertainment, they did not notice that the door behind them was slowly pulled open to a crack. A very thin and ugly man peered round it and watched the two fencers with one glaring eye. He stood there for quite a while, a queer, gangling figure, melting into the shadow behind him. Then he stepped back and closed the door noiselessly.

When the two men stopped, their torsos were dripping with sweat. Chiao Tai threw the sticks to a groom and ordered him to take them to the bath.

There were no other bathers in the large, airy room. It had two pools surrounded by a rail of solid logs of polished pinewood, left its natural colour. The walls were made of the same material, which filled the bathroom with a pleasant out-door scent. The floor was paved with large black tiles. The sturdy attendant, wearing only a loin cloth, took their trousers and hung them on the rack. Then he gave each a small cotton bag filled with a mixture of chaff and lye, and a round tub with hot water. Judge Dee and Chiao Tai scrubbed themselves with the soap-bags. When the attendant was throwing buckets of hot water over them he said :

' You'll like the pool, it has been hewn right from the rock this inn is built on. The hot water comes from the spring

17

underneath. Mind your feet—the stones in the left corner are burning hot.'

The two men stepped over the rail and went down into the pool. The attendant pushed the sliding doors open so that they could enjoy the view of the green banana leaves in the small walled-in garden outside. For a good while Judge Dee and Chiao Tai let themselves soak contentedly in the hot water. Then they sat on the low bamboo bench and had the attendant massage their shoulders, and rub their bodies dry. He gave them linen jackets, and they walked back to their room, completely refreshed.

They had just changed into their own robes and sat down for a cup of tea, when the door opened and a thin, one-eyed man stepped inside.

'That's the rascal we saw in the teahouse!' Chiao Tai exclaimed.

Judge Dee looked annoyed at the repulsive face. He said sourly:

'One usually knocks before entering a room. What do you want?'

'Just a few words with you, Mr . . . Shen.'

'What's your business?' the judge asked. He couldn't place this weird man at all.

'Practically the same as yours! I am a professional thief.'

'Shall I kick him out?' Chiao Tai asked angrily.

'Wait!' Judge Dee said. He was curious to know what all this meant. 'Since you know my name, my friend, you must also know that I am a commission agent.'

The other laughed scornfully.

'Shall I tell you what you really are, the pair of you?'

'Please do!' the judge said affably.

'Do you want the whole story?' the one-eyed man asked again.

'Certainly!' Judge Dee said. The man was intriguing him.

JUDGE DEE AND CHIAO TAI TAKE A BATH

'First, as to you with your beard and your smug face, you smell of the tribunal. Since you are a strong fellow, you must be a former headman of constables. You tortured an innocent prisoner to death, you filched money from the cashbox, or both. Anyway, you had to flee and you took to the road. Your mate is of course a professional highway robber. You work together, you with your solemn face and oily speech strike up acquaintance with unwary travellers, and your mate knocks them down. Now you two have decided you will go for bigger things, and you came down to the city to rob a jewellery shop. But let me tell you two country bumpkins that you'll never get anywhere in the city. Even a child can see that you are crooks!'

Chiao Tai wanted to get up but Judge Dee raised his hand. 'The fellow is quite entertaining!' he said. 'Tell me, what makes you think that we want to commit a burglary in this city?'

The ugly man sighed.

'All right!' he said with exaggerated patience. 'I'll give you a lesson, gratis, for nothing! This afternoon, when that bully there entered the teahouse, I recognized him of course immediately as a highway robber. His build, the way he walks, even I with my one eye could see that. He probably is originally an army deserter, by the way. There's a soldier-like air in the way he carries his shoulders. Then you arrived, I first thought you were a dismissed court clerk. Later I watched you stick-fencing—and damned fools you were to give yourselves away like that!—and I noticed that you also are a hefty bully, but that your skin is white and smooth. So I corrected myself, and placed you as a headman on the run. Well, as if all that were not yet enough, you announced yourselves as strangers by studying a guide-book of this town, and gloated together over the list of jewellers. So you see what beginners you are. I only wonder why you grew that dirty beard. To ape your magistrate, I suppose!'

'The fellow ceases to amuse me!' Judge Dee said calmly to Chiao Tai. 'Throw him out!'

Chiao Tai jumped up, but he was not quick enough. Like a flash of lightning the thin man had turned to the door, opened it and slipped through, closing it in Chiao Tai's face so that he bumped his head against the wooden panel. He cursed heartily and jerked the door open again. 'I'll get that son of a dog!' he growled.

'Halt!' Judge Dee called out. 'Come back! We can't have a scene here!'

As Chiao Tai sat down again, angrily rubbing his forehead, the judge continued with a faint smile:

'That insolent rascal was useful in so far as he reminded me of an important rule which a detector of crimes should always keep in mind. And that is that one should never let oneself be tempted to cling stubbornly to one theory. This is a clever and observant scoundrel. His reasoning about our identity was neatly done. But, once he had established his theory, he adapted every new fact to it, instead of testing whether those new facts should not make him revise his theory. He should have realized that our stick-fencing out in the open here could also mean that our position is so secure that we can indulge freely in activities that in others would raise suspicion. Well, I should be the last to criticize, though, for I made exactly the same mistake when I was investigating the gold murders in Peng-lai!'

'The bastard followed us from the teahouse!' Chiao Tai said. 'Why did he seek us out? He wouldn't have thought he could blackmail us, would he?'

'I hardly think so,' Judge Dee replied. 'He impresses me as a man who relies entirely on his wit and who is mortally afraid of physical violence. Well, we'll never see him again!

By the way, your mentioning the teahouse reminds me of those bits of conversation we overheard on the terrace there. About that queer suicide of a silk merchant called Ko, you remember? Let's stroll over to the tribunal and hear what it is all about. It's about time for the afternoon session to start.'

'Magistrate, you are on a holiday!' Chiao Tai said reproachfully.

'Yes, I am!' Judge Dee said with a bleak smile. 'But I must confess that I would like to see a bit more of my colleague Teng, without him knowing it. Further, I have presided over a tribunal so often that I would like to see the proceedings from the other side of the bench, for once. It'll be an instructive experience, for you also, my friend! On our way!'

In the hall the fat manager was busy adding up the bill of four merchants who were leaving. He had wound a white cloth round his sweating brow, and was industriously clicking the beads of his abacus. But he wasn't too busy to say, as the judge passed the counter:

'Behind the Temple of the War God you'll find a terrain especially reserved for physical exercise, Mr Shen.'

'Thank you,' the judge said primly, 'but I prefer to avail myself of the facilities offered by this hospitable inn.'

They went outside.

The two men made slow progress, for it had grown a little cooler, and a dense crowd was about. But when they crossed the open square in front of the tribunal compound, they saw no one near the gatehouse. Apparently the session had started already and the spectators were assembled in the court hall. They passed underneath the stone archway of the gatehouse, where hung the huge bronze gong that announced the beginning of each court session. The four guards sitting on the bench eyed them indifferently.

They hurriedly ran across the empty main courtyard and entered the shadowy hall. From far in the back they heard a monotonous voice droning a lengthy statement. The two men remained standing just inside the door, letting their eyes adjust themselves to the half darkness. Over the heads of the crowd of spectators standing together farther down, they saw against the back wall the high bench, covered with scarlet cloth, standing on a raised dais. Behind it was enthroned Magistrate Teng, resplendent in his official robe of shimmering green brocade, and wearing the black judge's cap, its two stiffened wings standing out on either side of his head. He seemed engrossed in the document in front of him, slowly tugging at his thin goatee. Counsellor Pan stood by the side of his chair, his hands folded in his sleeves. The magistrate's bench was flanked by two lower tables where the court clerks were sitting. Behind the one on the right stood a grey-haired man, evidently the senior scribe, reading aloud a legal document. The entire back wall of the hall was covered by a dark-violet screen-curtain. In its centre the large image of a unicorn, the symbol of perspicacity, was beautifully embroidered in gold thread.

Judge Dee went on and joined the crowd of spectators. Raising himself on tiptoe he could see four constables standing in front of the bench, carrying iron chains, clubs, hand screws and the other terrifying paraphernalia of their office. Their headman, a squat brutish-looking man with a thin ringbeard, stood somewhat apart, fingering a heavy whip. As usual everything in the tribunal was calculated to impress the public with the majesty of the law, and the awful consequences of getting involved with it. Everyone appearing there, old and young, rich and poor, and no matter whether complainant or accused, had to kneel on the bare stone floor in front of the bench, shouted at by the constables and, if the magistrate ordered so, cruelly beaten on the spot. For the

23

fundamental rule of justice was that everyone appearing before the bench was considered guilty until he was able to prove his innocence.

'We didn't miss much,' Judge Dee whispered to Chiao Tai. 'The scribe is reading out the new constitution of some guild or trade organization, I think he is coming to the concluding paragraphs.'

When, a little later, the scribe fell silent, the magistrate raised his head and spoke:

'You have all heard now the new text of the constitution of the Guild of Metal Workers, as submitted by the said guild and amended by this court. Is there any objection?' He waited a moment, surveying the audience. Judge Dee quickly ducked. When no one spoke up, Teng resumed: 'This court then declares that the new constitution is approved, and shall stand as such.'

He rapped the bench sharply with the gavel, an oblong block of hardwood significantly known as the 'Wood that frightens the hall'.

A rotund, middle-aged man with a large paunch stepped forward and knelt in front of the bench. He was clad in white mourning dress.

'Nearer!' the headman growled at him.

As the man in white obediently crawled closer to the dais, Judge Dee nudged his neighbour and asked:

'Who is that?'

'Don't you know? That's the banker Leng Chien. He is the associate of Ko Chih-yuan, the old silk merchant who committed suicide last night.'

'I see,' Judge Dee said. 'Who is he in mourning for?'

'Heaven, you don't know a thing, do you? He is in mourning for his younger brother, of course. The famous painter Leng Te, who died two weeks ago. It was that lingering lung disease of his that did it.'

24

MAGISTRATE TENG HEARS THE BANKER LENG CHIEN

Judge Dee nodded and concentrated his attention on what Leng Chien was saying.

'In accordance with Your Honour's instructions of this morning, we continued dragging the river for the deceased's body, as far as half a mile downstream. But we only retrieved his velvet cap. Since I am most anxious to begin winding up the affairs of the deceased on behalf of the Ko family, I take the liberty of reiterating my request made during the morning session of this court, namely that Your Honour have his demise officially registered, thus empowering me to act and sign documents on the deceased's behalf. There are a number of important deals pending which, if not immediately attended to, may cause serious financial loss to the estate.'

Magistrate Teng frowned. He said:

'The formalities must be complied with. The law states that a suicide cannot be registered unless the body has been brought forward for examination by a duly accredited coroner.' He thought for a while, then pursued: 'This morning you gave only a concise account of the occurrence. You shall now report what happened in detail. It is not impossible that this court may find circumstances which might motivate special consideration of the case. I am not oblivious of the fact that the late Mr Ko did have widespread financial interests, and I am willing to speed up the formalities as much as is possible within the limits of the law.'

'This person,' Leng said respectfully, 'is deeply grateful for Your Honour's kind consideration. Last night's dinner, during which the tragedy happened, was organized on the spur of the moment. One month ago Mr Ko consulted the famous soothsayer Pien Hoong about an auspicious date for beginning work on the summer villa Ko was planning to build in the southern suburb. When Mr Pien had drawn Ko's horoscope, he warned him that the fifteenth of this month, that is yesterday, would be a very dangerous date for him.

26

Greatly perturbed, Mr Ko pressed him for more details. But Pien could only add that the danger would originate in Ko's direct surroundings, and that it would be greatest at noon.

'Mr Ko who was by nature a nervous man, started to brood over this prediction, and suffered a renewal of an old stomach ailment of his. As the fateful date drew nearer he lost his appetite, and had to take medicine regularly for relieving his internal pains. I was greatly worried about him, and all through yesterday morning kept in touch with his steward. He said that Mr Ko had been very irritable all morning, and had refused to stir from the house, even for a walk in the garden. However, in the afternoon the steward sent me a message saying that his master's temper had considerably improved. He was happy that noon, the most dangerous hour, had passed without something untoward happening to him. Mrs Ko succeeded in persuading her husband to invite a few friends for dinner that night, to distract him and cheer him up. Ko invited, besides me, Mr Pan Yoo-te, Your Honour's counsellor, and the master of the guild of silk dealers.

'The dinner had been prepared in the garden pavilion of Mr Ko's residence. The pavilion stands at the farther end of the garden, on a slight elevation overlooking the river. At first Ko was in high spirits. He said jokingly that apparently even the famous soothsayer Pien Hoong sometimes made a mistake. When we were half through, however, he suddenly grew pale. He announced that he felt a severe stomach attack coming on. I said in jest that his nerves must be playing him false. He grew very angry and said that we were heartless fellows. He rose abruptly, muttering something about going over to the house to take his medicine.'

'How far is the pavilion from the house?' Magistrate Teng interrupted.

'The garden is quite large, Your Honour, but since it is planted only with shrubs, from the pavilion one can see clearly the marble terrace that runs along that side of the entire residence. It was on this moonlit terrace that, after a brief interval, we saw Ko reappear. His face was covered with blood, streaming from a wound on his forehead. Screaming and gesticulating wildly he ran down into the garden, and along the path towards the pavilion. The three of us sat there, looking at the approaching figure, speechless with consternation. Halfway down he suddenly changed his course. He left the path and ran across the grass to the marble balustrade. He stepped over it and threw himself into the river.'

The banker paused, overcome with emotion.

'What happened to the deceased while he was inside the house?' the magistrate asked.

'Precisely!' Judge Dee remarked to Chiao Tai. 'That's of course the crux of the matter!'

'Mrs Ko has stated,' Leng replied, 'that her husband came running inside their bedroom in great agitation. The bedroom is joined to the terrace by a narrow passage about ten feet long. He started upon a long tirade about the awful pain he was in, and the cruelty of his friends, who didn't show the slightest sympathy with his suffering. His wife tried to console him, then went to her own room to fetch his medicine. When she came back her husband had worked himself up into a kind of frenzy. Stamping his feet on the floor he refused to take the medicine. Suddenly he turned and rushed out to the terrace. That was the last his wife saw of him. I assume that, while running through the passage that leads to the terrace, he bumped his head against the upper part of the door. The passage is rather low. It was built after the rest of the house because Mr Ko wished to have direct access from his bedroom to the terrace. In the state of mind he was in, that unexpected shock completely unnerved him, and he decided to end his life.'

Magistrate Teng, who thus far had been listening with an indifferent air, now sat up in his chair. Turning round he asked his counsellor:

'Since you were there I assume that you examined the passage?'

'I did indeed, Your Honour,' Pan replied respectfully. 'I didn't find any bloodstains there, either on the floor or on the beam over the terrace door.'

'How high is the balustrade that runs along the river bank?' Teng asked the banker.

'Only three feet, Your Honour,' Leng Chien answered. 'I often advised Mr Ko to have it made higher, because there was the danger that some day a guest who had partaken too freely of the amber liquid might fall over. On the other side of the balustrade there's a sheer drop to the river, of more than ten feet, I'd say. But the deceased said he had made it low expressly in order to be able to enjoy the view while sitting in the garden.'

'How many steps lead up to the pavilion, and what kind are they?' Teng asked again.

'Three, Your Honour, and they are made of carved marble.'

'Did you see the deceased clearly when he went over into the river?'

Leng hesitated. He replied slowly:

'There are some shrubs there, and, since he had disappeared before we really knew what was happening, I ...'

Magistrate Teng leaned forward and interrupted:

'What made you think that Mr Ko committed suicide?'

'Good!' Judge Dee whispered to Chiao Tai. 'My colleague has put his finger on the sore spot!'

'The old fellow jumped into the river, didn't he?' Chiao Tai muttered. 'And evidently not to enjoy a swim!'

'Hush! Listen!' the judge hissed.

The banker seemed to be quite taken aback by Magistrate Teng's sudden question. He stammered:

'I . . . that is to say, all of us . . . since we saw it happen before our eyes . . .'

'You saw with your own eyes,' Magistrate Teng cut him short, 'that Mr Ko's face was covered with blood. That he first made straight for the pavilion, then changed direction and ran towards the balustrade. Didn't it occur to you that the blood from his head wound might have got into his eyes, and that he mistook the white balustrade for the white steps of the pavilion? And that he did not step over the balustrade, but stumbled over it?' As Leng did not reply, the magistrate continued: 'It has now become evident that the manner of Mr Ko's death has by no means been clearly established; this court provisionally opines that it was death by accident rather than suicide. Neither is this court satisfied with Mr Leng's theory about how the deceased received the head wound. Pending clarification of those issues, the death of Mr Ko Chih-yuan cannot be registered.'

He rapped his gavel and closed the session. When he had got up from his chair, Pan pulled the unicorn screen aside. Magistrate Teng passed through, going to the judge's private office, which is always located directly behind the court hall.

'Clear the hall!' the headman of the constables shouted at the spectators.

Judge Dee and Chiao Tai trooped towards the entrance with the crowd. The judge said:

'Teng is perfectly right, the evidence available so far could be interpreted as pointing to accident as well as to suicide. I wonder why that banker assumed straightaway that Ko committed suicide. I wonder also what actually happened to Ko when he was inside the house.'

'Nice riddles for Magistrate Teng to rack his brains on!' Chiao Tai said cheerfully. 'Now, what about sampling the local dishes?'

III

In the market place, teeming with a noisy crowd, they halted in front of a small eating-house that looked rather inviting. The row of large coloured lanterns hanging from the eaves was inscribed with the grandiloquent name of the restaurant: 'Roost of all Gourmets within the Four Seas'.

'Here we can hardly go wrong!' Judge Dee remarked smiling. He pulled aside the door curtain of clean blue cotton and was greeted by an appetizing smell of frying onions.

They had an excellent meal of rice, roast pork and pickled vegetables. Tasting the heady local wine, they talked about their adventures in the prefectural city, and then exchanged reminiscences about the past year at home, in Peng-lai. When they left the restaurant Judge Dee had lost his preoccupied air, and they strolled back to the hostel in the best of moods. Now and then they halted in a gaily lit shopping street, looking at the local products which were praised by vociferous street vendors, or listening in to a particularly acrimonious bout of bargaining.

While they were walking the judge noticed that Chiao Tai had grown rather quiet. 'What is wrong with you?' he asked. 'Doesn't the meal agree with you?'

'We are being followed!' Chiao Tai replied in a low voice.

'Who would follow us?' Judge Dee asked incredulously. 'Did you see them?'

'No, but I have a feeling for these things, and so far it has never failed me. Let's walk on, I'll try a few tricks to find out who is keeping an eye on us.'

He quickened his pace and turned into a less crowded side

street. As soon as he was around the corner he abruptly halted, pulling the judge with him into a dark porch. They scrutinized the passers-by. But they saw no face they knew, and no one seemed to take the slightest interest in them. They resumed their walk, now choosing dark back streets where only few people were about.

'It's no use,' Chiao Tai said when they were in a narrow alley. 'Whoever is spying on us is an old hand at the game. You'd better return to the hostel, Magistrate. Do you see the group of beggars blocking up the road ahead there, in front of that street stall? When we pass there I'll join them. You just turn that corner quickly. I'll see you in the hostel, and bring those dirty spies along for you!'

Judge Dee nodded. While he was elbowing his way through the group of ragged vagrants in front of the stall, Chiao Tai suddenly vanished from his sight. The judge slipped round the corner and ran through a few winding alleys, in the direction of the street noise ahead. Once in a crowded street again he asked the way to the hostel, and found it without difficulty.

The waiter brought tea and two candles. Judge Dee sat down at the small table. Sipping the hot tea he reflected that it seemed incredible that anyone would take a special interest in their doings. Yet Chiao Tai was rarely wrong in such matters. In his own district of Peng-lai there were of course a few scoundrels who were not very kindly disposed towards him, but even if some of them had the temerity to make an attempt on his life, how could they possibly know that he would break his journey here in Wei-ping? That idea had been formed only during his last day in the Prefecture. Or did a gang in Peng-lai perhaps have an accomplice there? He began to stroke his long beard pensively.

There was a knock on the door and Chiao Tai came in. Wiping the sweat from his brow he said dejectedly:

33

'Again he slipped through my fingers! You know who it is? None other than that ugly one-eyed bastard who came to see us this afternoon! I saw him slink past, looking left and right as if searching for someone. I was in the front row of those beggars, drinking a cup of the dregs that street stall sells, and while I was pushing the fellows aside to get at him, he spotted me and off he went like a hare! I ran after him, but he was nowhere to be seen!'

'He's a slippery customer,' the judge said. 'I wonder what he is up to. Have you by any chance seen the fellow before, either in Peng-lai or in the Prefecture?'

Chiao Tai shook his head. As the judge motioned him to be seated also he replied:

'If I had ever seen that ugly snout I would certainly remember it! But don't worry, now I know whom to look for. He'll certainly try to follow us again when we go out, and then I'll get him. By the way, your colleague Teng here has another worry coming, Magistrate! A murdered woman!'

'What is that?' the judge asked astonished. 'Did you see it happen?'

'No,' Chiao Tai said, 'but it's murder all right! As yet known only to an old beggar and me!'

'Out with it!' Judge Dee ordered curtly. 'What happened? We'll have to report immediately to Teng.'

'We might be doing him a good turn,' Chiao Tai agreed. He poured himself a cup of tea, then began: 'It was like this. After that thin scoundrel had disappeared, I went back to the street stall to pay my coppers. As I turn to go, a dirty old beggar sidles up to me and asks whether he's right in assuming that I am a stranger in town. When I say yes and what is it to you, he pulls me aside and asks whether I'd be interested in buying some fine jewellery extra cheap. I think I may as well see what it's all about, so I let him take me to the porch of a quack doctor round the corner. Under the door-lampion he shows me a pair of beautiful earrings and two golden bracelets, and says I can have them then and there for one silver piece. I know of course that the old geezer has filched the trinkets, and I am debating with myself whether I'll take him here first, or straight to the tribunal. He thinks I am hesitating because I am afraid to buy the stuff, and he says, "Don't worry, there won't be any trouble. I took them from a dead woman lying in the marsh near the north gate. I am the only one who knows about it." I tell him to come across with the whole story, and he says he has a lair in the shrubs on the edge of the marsh, where he sleeps sometimes. He went there tonight and came upon the dead body of a youngish woman, dressed in a fine brocade coat, half-hidden under the shrubbery. The hilt of a dagger was sticking from her breast, and she was quite dead. He felt in the sleeves but there was no money, so he tore off her earrings, took the bracelets, and ran off. That place is quite deserted at night, there was nobody about. Now, as a regular member of the beggars' guild, he's supposed to give everything he finds or steals to the boss of the underworld here, a ruffian called The Corporal, who then gives him a share. The old rascal says he thought it a pity to let go of such nice loot, therefore he was looking for a stranger who'd buy it, without the risk of him being betrayed to The Corporal—for whom he has an unholy fear.'

'Where is this beggar?' Judge Dee asked. 'Don't tell me that he slipped through your fingers too!'

Chiao Tai scratched his head. 'No,' he replied with an embarrassed air, 'he didn't. But the fact is that the fellow looked half-starved. He really was a rather pathetic old wreck. I questioned him up and down, and I am absolutely certain that he has nothing to do with that murder. I examined the earrings, and found some dried blood on them, so he didn't

35

lie about taking them from a corpse. I know what 'll happen to him if we take the poor wretch to the tribunal! The constables 'll beat him up, and if and when they let him go that Corporal 'll cut him to ribbons for not having brought the loot to him. I know the gentle manners of his sort! So I dig out a string of coppers, give them to him and tell him to run along. I thought that when we go to report this to your colleague in the tribunal, you might say that the beggar we got the baubles from ran away.'

Judge Dee gave his lieutenant a thoughtful look.

'It's very irregular, of course,' he said after a while, 'but I can see your point. An old beggar has no chance to get inside a gentlewoman's mansion, and when she is going out she rides in a litter and is well attended. And the beggar must have spoken the truth also when he said there was no one about, else he wouldn't have dared to rob the body. The woman was evidently murdered somewhere else, and her dead body deposited in the marsh. No, I don't think that in this case you did much harm. But don't let your good heart get the better of you too often, Chiao Tai! We'll now go straight to the tribunal; Magistrate Teng must initiate the investigation without delay.' Rising he added: 'Let me have a look at those things!'

Chiao Tai reached into his sleeve and laid two earrings and two glittering bracelets on the table. Judge Dee gave them a casual look. 'Good workmanship!' he commented. He was about to turn to the door when he suddenly checked himself. He stooped, pulled the candle closer, and scrutinized the jewels intently. Each earring consisted of a small lotus flower, moulded in silver, in an elaborate gold-filigree setting, studded with six rubies, small but of excellent quality. The bracelets were of solid gold and had the shape of snakes. The eyes were large green emeralds that glowed in the candle light with a malicious glare. Judge Dee righted himself. He remained

36

standing there staring at the jewels, slowly pulling at his moustache.

After a while Chiao Tai asked anxiously:

'Well, don't you think we'd better be on our way?'

The judge took the jewels up and put them in his sleeve. Looking at Chiao he said gravely:

'I think we had better not report this to Magistrate Teng, Chiao Tai. Not just yet.'

Chiao Tai shot him an astonished look. But just as he was about to ask what the judge meant, the door opened and the thin man came rushing inside. He said excitedly:

'They have caught up with you! And even sooner than I thought! You were crazy to visit the tribunal! The headman is in front, asking what room you have. But don't worry, I'll help you escape. Follow me!'

Chiao Tai was about to make an angry retort, but the judge raised his hand. He hesitated just a moment, then said to the ugly man: 'Lead the way!'

He took them outside and quickly dragged them into a narrow corridor. He seemed to be entirely familiar with the hostel's layout. He led them into a pitch-dark, smelly passage, then opened a ramshackle door. They found themselves in a dark alleyway. Their guide picked his way among heaps of refuse. The smell of frying fat indicated that they were somewhere behind the hostel's kitchen. Farther along the thief entered another door. It proved to be the back entrance of the large winehouse next door. He elbowed his way through the noisy crowd of customers to the front door, then took them through a maze of streets and alleys, some going up, others down, now to the right, then to the left. Soon the judge had lost all sense of direction.

Then the thief halted, so suddenly that Judge Dee collided with him. They stood at the entrance of a dismal back street.

He pointed at the only lighted window at the opposite end of the street and said:

'That's the Phoenix Inn. You'll be perfectly safe there. Tell the Corporal that Kun-shan sent you. You'll see me later.' He turned round, skilfully slipped past Chiao Tai, who tried to grab him, and disappeared into the darkness.

IV

Chiao Tai cursed violently. He said sourly:

'I do hope you have a good reason for all this, Magistrate! For let me warn you that, in spite of its poetical name, that inn over there must be the headquarters of the boss of the underworld here!'

'I am certain it is just that,' Judge Dee said calmly. 'If we find that the Corporal is involved in some dirty scheme together with our one-eyed friend, we'll at least discover what is behind their interest in us, and if necessary fight our way out. If not, then the Corporal and his crowd are exactly the people I need for solving a queer problem that is rather worrying me. In any case we'll begin by acting the part Mr Kun-shan so kindly assigned to us, namely that of highway robbers. Come on!'

Chiao Tai grinned. Tightening his belt he said:

'Maybe we'll have a good fight there!'

They walked on to the house, a ramshackle two-storeyed building of wooden boards. Through the lighted window came the sound of rough voices. When Chiao Tai knocked on the door, the murmur within suddenly ceased. The grated peephole opened and a gruff voice asked:

'Who is it?'

'Two men coming for the Corporal!' Chiao Tai growled.

There was the sound of a crossbar being removed. A slovenly clad man let them inside a large, low-ceilinged room that smelled of stale sweat and cheap liquor. It was dimly lit by one smoking oil-lamp. The fellow was apparently the waiter, for he went straight to the high counter in the rear.

Ensconced behind it he moodily looked the two men over, then muttered:

'The boss hasn't come yet.'

'We'll wait!' the judge said and walked over to a small table by the window. He sat down heavily on the chair facing the room. Chiao Tai seated himself opposite, scowled over his shoulder at the waiter and shouted:

'Two wine here. Of the best!'

Four men who had been gambling at the larger table in the far corner near the counter eyed them suspiciously for a while, then resumed their game. A slatternly young woman who stood at the counter looked them up and down with an insolent stare. She wore a long black skirt and a red sash round her waist, and on top a loose dark-green jacket that left her shapely bosom bare. A wilted red rose was stuck in her hair. Her scrutiny completed, she began to whisper to the youngster next to her. He had a rather handsome but dissolute face. The young man shrugged, pushed the girl roughly away, and turned round to watch the gambling, leaning his back against the counter.

One of the gamblers, a thin man with a ragged moustache, let the dice rattle in the coconut shell, then threw. He announced in a sing-song voice:

'A pair of fours, four cross-eyed whores!'

The next, a broad-shouldered, completely bald man scooped up the dice. After he had thrown them he shouted with a curse:

'A three and a six! The damned luck I am having to-night!'

'You must try to play the game more often!' the youngster at the counter sneered.

'Shut up, Student!' the bald man growled. The fourth player threw the dice. Slamming his hand on the table he called out:

40

'A pair of eights, two leaking crates, they walked the street, and still found mates! The pool is for me!'

The waiter placed two wine-cups on Judge Dee's table. 'That'll be six coppers!' he said in a surly voice.

The judge laboriously counted out four coppers on the table. 'I never pay more than two apiece,' he announced.

'Halve the difference or clear out!' the waiter said.

Judge Dee gave him an additional copper. As the man went, the judge said loudly to Chiao Tai: 'The dirty crook!'

The waiter turned round angrily.

'Want to make something of that, bastard?' Chiao Tai asked invitingly. The waiter decided not to take up the challenge.

Loud curses came from the other end of the room. The bald man shouted at the youngster:

'Keep out of our game, I tell you! You're too green even to steal from a monk's almsbowl, you don't even have a few coppers to gamble with. Keep your trap shut, Mister Student!'

'The only cash the runt has is what the wench here gives to him,' the second gambler remarked. And, to the Student: 'If the Corporal gets to know about that, you're in for it, dirty pimp!'

The young man went for him with balled fists. But before he had reached the speaker, the bald gambler had stopped him with a hard blow to his stomach that made him reel back gasping against the counter. The four gamblers guffawed. The girl uttered a cry and ran over to the youngster. She kept her arm round his shoulders while he vomited into the spittoon. When he had righted himself, his face deadly pale, she clutched at his sleeve and whispered something. 'Leave me alone, you stupid slut!' he panted. Then he slapped her face. She went behind the counter and began to sob, hiding her face in her sleeve.

'Pleasant company!' Judge Dee remarked to Chiao Tai. The latter was looking sadly at the wine-cup in his hand. He muttered:

'This is even worse than the rotgut I got at the street stall!' Then he turned round and watched the girl for a while. She had now wiped her face and was leaning on the counter, staring straight ahead. 'If you'd scrape off all that rouge and powder,' Chiao Tai remarked judiciously, 'she wouldn't be a bad-looking wench. Good figure, anyway.'

The young man had recovered. Suddenly he pulled a knife from his belt. But the waiter reached out over the counter, grabbed his hand from behind and gave it a quick twist. The knife clattered to the floor. 'You know the boss doesn't want knife-fighting, runt!' the waiter told him placidly.

The bald man had risen and picked up the knife. Now he raked the youngster's face with a nasty back-hand blow. The Student's face was suddenly covered with blood.

'So you've been in a knife fight already today, eh?' the bald man said with satisfaction. 'They gave you a good cut across your forehead. Children shouldn't play with knives!'

Two hard knocks resounded on the door.

'That's the boss!' the bald man said and went quickly to open.

A squat, hulking man came in. He had a broad, coarse face with a ragged ringbeard and a short, bristling moustache. His greying hair was bound up with a piece of cloth, and he wore wide blue trousers and a kind of waistcoat that left his deep, hairy chest and muscular arms bare. He ignored the bald man's respectful greeting and walked straight to the counter, without looking right or left.

'A large bowl, from my special jar!' he barked at the waiter. 'Just had a little affair, a narrow squeeze, I tell you! How can a man make a decent living in this blooming town?

42

THE TAPROOM OF THE PHOENIX INN

Everywhere you run into those rats from the tribunal!' He gulped down the wine, smacked his lips and shouted at the girl: 'Don't stand there blubbering, wench!' And, to the waiter: 'Give her a drink too, mate! Life ain't always easy for her either!'

His eyes fell on the young man, who was wiping the blood off his face. 'What's wrong with the Student?' the Corporal asked.

'He drew a knife on me, boss!' the bald man said.

'He did, did he? Come here, runt!'

As the frightened youngster came up to him with lagging steps, the Corporal gave him a contemptuous look and asked with a sneer:

'So you like knife-fighting, eh? All right, show me what you can do!'

A long, gleaming knife appeared in the Corporal's hand. With his left he grabbed the Student's collar. The waiter ducked under the counter, but the girl leaned over quickly and laid her hand on the Corporal's shoulder.

'Let him go, please!' she cried out desperately.

The Corporal shook his shoulder free. He had now seen the two men by the window. He pushed the trembling Student roughly out of his way, stepped forward and exclaimed: 'Holy Heaven! Who's the beard?'

'Strangers, boss!' the Student said obsequiously. 'Just came in.'

The waiter popped up again behind the counter. He said venomously:

'That beard called me a crook, boss!'

'Nobody ever said you weren't! But I don't trust blasted strangers.' The Corporal walked over to Judge Dee's table and asked gruffly: 'Where are you from?'

'We got into a bit of trouble,' Judge Dee replied, 'and Kun-shan sent us here.'

44

The Corporal gave them a dubious look. He pulled up a chair to the table, sat down and said:

'I don't know Kun-shan too well. Tell me about the trouble!'

'Me and my mate,' the judge answered, 'are simple businessmen trying hard to make an honest living along the road. This morning we met a merchant out in the mountains. He took a liking to us and gave us ten silver pieces to remember him by. Then he laid himself down by the roadside to take a nap, and we went on to town to invest our money. But that merchant woke up in a nasty temper, the crook ran to the tribunal and said we had robbed him. The constables came for us, and Kun-shan took us here. It was nothing but a slight misunderstanding, based on that merchant waking up too soon.'

'That's a good one!' the Corporal said with a grin. Then he asked, suspicious again: 'Why do you drag along that beard with you? And why do you talk like a schoolmaster?'

'That beard,' Chiao Tai said, 'he let grow to please his boss. He used to be a headman of constables in the olden days, but he had to retire before he had earned his pension, because of some financial misunderstanding. By the way, are you an ex-headman too? You seem in the habit of asking questions!'

'I have to make sure, don't I?' the Corporal said sourly. 'And don't call me names, you! Ex-headman nothing! I am from the army. Corporal Liu of the Third Wing of the Western Army. Get that into your thick skull, will you?' And, to the judge: 'Is Kun-shan an old friend of yours?'

'No,' Judge Dee answered, 'we met him for the first time today. He happened to be there when the law came for us.'

'Good!' the Corporal grunted. 'Have a drink on the house!' He shouted at the waiter, who came running with a wine-jar. When they had tasted the wine, the Corporal asked:

'Where were you last?'

'In Peng-lai,' the judge replied. 'We didn't like it there.'

'Stands to reason!' the Corporal grinned. 'I have heard about the new thief-catcher-in-chief they have got there, fellow called Dee, the nastiest cross-patch in the whole province! A week ago he had the head of a friend of mine chopped off.'

'That's why we left. We used to stay with the Butcher, in his inn near the north gate.'

The Corporal crashed his large fist on the table.

'Why didn't you say so at once, brother? That bastard Kun-shan hasn't got a patch on the Butcher! Straight-forward man, the Butcher was. A bit short-tempered, maybe, much too ready with his knife. Told him a hundred times that that's a bad mistake.'

Judge Dee was glad that the Corporal concurred in his verdict. The Butcher had treacherously stabbed a man to death, and he had sentenced him just before leaving Peng-lai for the Prefecture. He asked: 'Does Kun-shan belong to your organization?'

'No, he is a kind of independent worker. A high-class burglar, very good at his job, I am told. But he's a mean, cantankerous bastard, I am glad he doesn't come here too often. You two are all right, though. Have to be, since you stayed with the Butcher. Put a string of coppers in our pool, and you are welcome to stay with us here.'

Judge Dee took a string from his sleeve. The Corporal threw it across the taproom to the bald man, who caught it dexterously.

'We would like to stay here a few days,' the judge said, 'till the hue and cry has died down, so to speak.'

'That's settled then,' the Corporal said. He shouted at

the girl: 'Come over here, Carnation! Meet two new lodgers!'

As she came to the table the Corporal put his arm round her waist and said to the judge:

'This is our housekeeper. She is an ex-professional, but still as good as new, eh, Carnation? Nowadays she only walks the street if she needs a new dress or so, amateur-like. I share her with Baldy, because he is my number two, you see, and since we share the money too.' He looked thoughtfully at the judge, then asked suddenly: 'Can you read and write?' As Judge Dee nodded he went on with enthusiasm: 'Why don't you stay here longer, brother? You can have a room upstairs, drink down here, and if you get troubled by your human nature, I don't mind you taking Carnation through her paces, now and then. Don't look cross now, my wench, you'll get accustomed to that beard!' He pinched the pouting girl, then went on: 'You don't know the brain-work I have to do here, brother! I have more than seventy beggars and vagabonds working under me, and they come here every other night for the reckoning. Twenty per cent for me, ten for Baldy, and ten for the house. And, being no man of letters, I have to figure it all out with dots and crosses! That Student there could help me, only the men won't have it, they don't trust him yet. I'd let you start at five per cent, and what you earn yourself is tax-free. Speak up, is it a deal?'

'It's a generous offer,' the judge answered, 'but I think I'd better pass on as soon as I can. I don't hold with murder, you know.'

The Corporal pushed the girl away. Putting his large fists on his knees he asked tensely:

'Murder, you say? Where?'

'I heard a man at the market say that there's a murdered woman lying in the marsh. My mate and I do only robbery.

47

We find it pays better, in the long run. Murder always means trouble. Big trouble.'

'Baldy!' bellowed the Corporal. And, as the bald man came running: 'Why didn't you report to me that there's a murdered woman lying around, eh? Who did it?'

'I don't know nothing about a murdered woman, boss, I swear it!' the bald man whined. 'Nobody told me about it!'

'Shall I go out there and see whether it's true?' the judge asked.

'It wouldn't be you who slit her throat, would it now?' the Corporal asked threateningly.

'Would I go back there if I had done it?' Judge Dee asked with scorn.

'No, you wouldn't, I suppose,' the Corporal muttered. He rubbed his low, corrugated forehead, looking morosely at his wine-cup.

The judge got up and said:

'Give me a man to take me there by the back streets, and I'll have a look. Don't forget that I've been a headman, I know all about dead bodies. Perhaps I can find out for you who did it too!'

The Corporal hesitated. After a while he looked up and said:

'All right, take the Student. I can't let the others go. Soon my men will be coming in for the accounts. Hey, Student, you go with the beard!'

'You better stay here, mate!' Judge Dee said to Chiao Tai. 'The two of us together might attract the attention of the thief-catchers.'

Chiao Tai had followed the conversation in speechless astonishment. He grunted something, then took the wine-jar and hurriedly refilled his cup.

V

The Student took Judge Dee along some less frequented streets and alleys down to the northern section of the town. He explained that the Phoenix Inn was located in the hilly, central quarter. The town was built on the mountain slope, and the northern quarter was the lowest part. The judge didn't say much. He was preoccupied with his own thoughts. It was clear that the Corporal knew nothing about the murder or about Kun-shan's plans. A number of facts pointed to his theory being right, yet . . .

'Do many people pass that marsh during the day?' he suddenly asked the young man.

'Yes, in the morning there's a lot of traffic there,' the Student replied. 'The peasants come in from the plain beyond the north gate, bringing vegetables and so on for the market. But at night it's a very lonely place. They say it's haunted.'

'Why didn't the authorities have the marsh filled up?'

'We had a big earthquake four years ago, I was fourteen then, I remember it well. It was especially bad in the north quarter, and it destroyed the houses built where the marsh now is. There was a fire. Heaven, you should have seen it, it was a beauty! People with their clothes burning came rushing to the river, screaming their heads off, I never laughed so much in my life! A pity the fire didn't get to the tribunal, though! Well, later, when they started to clear the ruins, they found that the ground there had sunk below river level, it was too soggy to build there. So they let it lie waste, and now it's overgrown with weeds and shrubs.'

Judge Dee nodded. He reflected that a region which has many hot springs often suffers from earthquakes.

They were passing through a narrow, quiet street. The curved roofs of the dark houses stood out against the moonlit sky.

'I would like to leave that gang of the Corporal's, you know,' the Student resumed.

The judge shot him a quick look. He had thought him a rather offensive specimen, but apparently he had done him an injustice.

'Would you now?' he remarked non-committally.

'Of course!' the Student said scornfully. 'You can see that I am quite different from that riff-raff, can't you? My father was a schoolmaster, I got a good education, graduated from the town school. I ran away because I wanted to become something really big. But the Corporal's was the only gang I could join in this town. Petty thieving and begging, that's all they do! And the stupid dogs are always taunting me, just because they know I am a better man than they are!'

'I see,' Judge Dee said.

'You and your mate are different,' the Student went on wistfully. 'I dare say you two have slit a few throats! You only told the Corporal you didn't like murder because you heard the waiter say that the Corporal won't have killings in this town. Don't worry about me, I can put two and two together!'

'Is it still far?' the judge asked.

'Next street. It comes to a dead-end behind the tribunal, where the ruined houses are. Say, did you often torture women when you were still headman?'

'Let's hurry!' Judge Dee said curtly.

'I wager they squealed like pigs when you put the hot irons to them! All women go for me, you know, but I have no use for them, the stupid bitches! When they put them on the rack, they also crush their arms in screws, don't they? Do they scream a lot?'

The judge gripped the Student's elbow in a wrestler's lock. His iron fingers dug deep into the flesh and nerves. The Student yelled frantically until Judge Dee released him.

'You dirty bully!' the youngster sobbed, supporting his bruised arm with the other.

'You asked a question, didn't you?' the judge said affably. 'Now you have supplied yourself the correct answer!'

Silently they picked their way among half-ruined, deserted houses. They came out on a wide, open space. A hot grey mist hovered low over a stretch of small trees and thick undergrowth. Farther on loomed the crenellated watch-tower of the north city gate.

'That's your marsh!' the Student announced sullenly.

It was very still. The din of the busy shopping streets farther uptown did not penetrate here. There were only the eery cries of waterfowl.

Judge Dee followed the slippery footpath that seemed to run round the marsh, peering intently among the low shrubs. Then he halted. He had seen a patch of red, shimmering under the bushes. He quickly went up to it, his boots squelching in the mud. He parted the branches. A dead body was lying there, wrapped from neck to feet in a sumptuous long coat of red brocade with a golden flower pattern.

Stooping he studied the still face for a moment, looking silently at the regular, handsome features and the curious, completely serene expression of the dead woman. Her extraordinarily long hair, of a strange silken beauty, had been clumsily bound up by means of a coarse cotton band. He put her age at about twenty-five. The earlobes were torn, but only a very few drops of blood were visible. He opened the coat, then quickly closed it again.

'Go down the path and watch!' he brusquely ordered the Student. 'Whistle if you see somebody coming!'

As the young man slunk away, the judge folded the coat back. The woman was completely naked. A dagger had been buried to the hilt under her left breast, and around it was a patch of dried blood. Scrutinizing the hilt, of beautifully chased silver but blackened by age, he decided that it was a valuable antique. The beggar hadn't recognized it as such, and therefore he hadn't taken it when he stole the earrings and the bracelets. He felt the breast. It was clammy. Then he lifted one of the arms, and found it was still limp. The woman had been murdered only a few hours before, he thought. The serene face, the clumsily gathered wealth of hair, the naked body and the bare feet pointed to her having been killed while she was in bed and asleep. Then the murderer had hastily bound up the hair, wrapped the body in the coat, and brought it out here. That fitted well with his reasoning.

He pushed aside the branches overhead and let the moonlight fall on the slim body. He sat back on his haunches, rolled up his sleeves and carefully examined the lower part of the corpse. He had a wide knowledge of medicine, including the special science of the coroner. As he wiped off his hands on the wet grass, his face bore a perplexed expression. The woman had been raped. That upset his entire theory! He stood up and wrapped the body in the red coat again, then dragged it farther under the overhanging branches so that it could not be seen from the path. He walked back.

The Student was sitting hunched on a large boulder, nursing his elbow. 'I can hardly move it!' he muttered.

'You distress me!' Judge Dee said coldly. 'Wait here for me. I am going to search those houses over there.'

'Please don't leave me alone here!' the youngster whined.

52

'They say the ghosts of the people who died here during the fire still haunt this place!'

'That's bad!' the judge said. 'You said just now that their cries amused you. The ghosts will have heard that. But wait, I'll help you!' He walked three times round the boulder with measured pace, muttering some weird spells under his breath. 'You are safe!' he announced. 'I learned to make that magic circle from an old itinerant Taoist monk. No ghost can come inside.'

He left, convinced that the youngster wouldn't meddle with the dead body while he was away.

After he had made his way through the ruins, he came on a row of inhabited houses. On the next street-corner he saw the lighted lampions of the teahouse where he had been sitting that afternoon with Chiao Tai. A short walk brought him to the back door of the tribunal compound. He knocked.

VI

Sooner than he had expected the door opened. The old steward said with evident relief:

'So you did get the message our headman left in the hostel! My master has been waiting up for you, Mr Shen, hoping that you would come.'

He led the judge straight to Magistrate Teng's library. They found him dozing in the armchair behind his desk. The light of two large silver candelabra shone on his shrunken face. When the steward had woken him up, he rose quickly and came round the desk to meet the judge. He waited till the steward had left, then exclaimed agitatedly:

'Thank Heaven that you came! I am in an awful predicament, Dee! I badly need your advice. Take a seat, please!'

When they had sat down at the tea-table, Judge Dee said:

'I presume that it concerns the murder of your wife.'

'How did you know?' Magistrate Teng asked aghast.

'I'll first tell you what I know. Then you'll explain what happened.'

Teng raised his teacup with a shaking hand, spilling some tea on the polished table top.

'When I visited you this afternoon,' Judge Dee began, 'I couldn't help noticing how ill and perturbed you were. Concerned about you, I later asked Pan Yoo-te what was ailing you, but he said that you had been perfectly all right in the morning. Thus I knew that you must have had a severe shock, just before my arrival. I remembered that when your steward inquired about your wife, you said that during the siesta she had unexpectedly received a summons to go and visit her elder sister. But the steward had said that her bed-

54

room door was locked. That struck me as curious. Why should your wife have locked her bedroom when she left? Surely the maids would have to go there to make the bed and so on? At the same time the steward informed you that an antique vase in your wife's ante-room had been broken. You took that news very calmly, yet Pan told me afterwards that it was a costly heirloom which you valued highly. Evidently you knew already about that mishap, and more important things than a broken vase were weighing on your mind. Thus I concluded that during the siesta something must have happened in your wife's bedroom that greatly upset you. Since, however, your household affairs are no concern of mine, I didn't give those matters further thought.'

The judge took a sip of his tea. As Magistrate Teng remained silent, he pursued:

'Then fortuitous circumstances placed in my hands some jewellery which a beggar had stolen from the dead body of a woman, said to be lying out in the marsh. Among those jewels was a pair of earrings, silver lotus flowers, in a very elaborate, costly setting of gold and rubies. Since the value of the setting must be twenty or thirty times that of the silver lotus flowers, evidently the motif of the lotus had a special meaning. I feared that they belonged to your wife, whose name is Silver Lotus. Of course I couldn't be certain that there wasn't another lady in this town called Silver Lotus, but remembering your agitation and the curious sudden departure of your wife, I suspected that there was a connection.

'Just when I had arrived at that conclusion, your headman came to the hostel asking for me. I assumed you wanted to consult me. But I felt that, before seeing you, I must learn more about the murdered woman. Therefore I hurriedly left the hostel by the back door, and found someone who took me to the marsh. I examined the body. There could be no doubt that she was a gentlewoman, while the fact that she wore no clothes pointed to her having been killed in her bed. The condition of the body confirmed that death had occurred during the siesta hour. Since the marsh is near the tribunal, I concluded that the dead body was indeed that of your wife, killed during the siesta in her bedroom, and after dark deposited in the marsh. This is an unfrequented neighbourhood at night, and in addition your residence has a secret exit to the usually deserted back street, so that the body could be transported with small risk. Am I right?'

'All your deductions are quite correct, Dee,' the magistrate said slowly. 'But . . .'

Judge Dee raised his hand.

'Before you say anything further I wish to state that no matter what happened here, I'll do everything I can to help you. But don't expect me to transgress the law, or to impede the course of justice. Therefore I warn you that if you choose to give an explanation, I'll have to consider that as evidence, and shall quote it in court if summoned as a witness. It is for you to decide whether we continue this conversation or not.'

'I quite understand,' Magistrate Teng said in a toneless voice. 'Of course this terrible tragedy must be brought before the Prefect. But you'll help me greatly by letting me tell you everything, and by advising me as to how to formulate my defence. For it was indeed I who killed my wife.'

'Why?' Judge Dee asked quietly.

The magistrate leaned back in his chair. He said wearily: 'The answer to that question goes back a long way. More than seventy years.'

'I put your age at not more than forty, and that of your wife at twenty-five!' the judge said astonished.

Magistrate Teng nodded. He asked:

'Are you by any chance a student of military history,

Dee? In that case you may be familiar with the name Teng Kuo-yao.'

Judge Dee knitted his bushy eyebrows.

'Teng Kuo-yao . . .' he said pensively. 'Let me see now. There was an able general of that name, he earned fame by his bravery in our great campaign in Central Asia. A brilliant future at Court was predicted for him, but he suddenly went into retirement because . . .' The judge stopped abruptly and gave his host a startled look. 'Heaven, was the general your grandfather?'

Teng nodded slowly.

'He was. And allow me to state in plain terms what you hesitated to pronounce just now. He had to retire early because in a fit of temporary insanity he stabbed his best friend to death. He was acquitted, but had of course to resign.'

Deep silence reigned in the room. After a while the magistrate resumed:

'My father was a perfectly healthy and normal man. Why should I have assumed that the disease was hereditary? Eight years ago I married Silver Lotus. I don't think there often are found a man and wife so completely, so unreservedly devoted to each other. If I acquired the reputation of being rather unsociable, it was because no company could be dearer to me than that of my beloved wife. Then one day, now seven years ago, my wife found me lying unconscious on the floor of my bedroom. When I came to I was ill. Strange memories flitted through my fevered brain. After long hesitation, I told my wife the truth. During that fit I had dreamt I savagely murdered a man, and revelled in that gory deed. I told her that a hereditary curse was on me, that she couldn't go on living with a madman, and that I would do everything to arrange for a speedy divorce.'

He covered his face with his hands. Judge Dee looked with

deep compassion at the stricken man. When the magistrate had mastered his emotion, he went on:

'Silver Lotus resolutely refused. She said she would never leave me, that she would look after me and see to it that nothing untoward happened, should I have other attacks—if I did have them, for she added that nobody could say whether my fit hadn't been due to other causes. I protested, but when she insisted, saying that she would kill herself if I divorced her, at last I, miserable wretch, gave in. . . . We had no children yet, and we decided there should be none. We hoped that our literary work together would make us forget that we were compelled to forgo the joy of seeing the fruits of our conjugal love. If I seemed to the outside world a reserved, rather cold man, Dee, I hope you'll now understand the reason.'

Judge Dee nodded silently. There was little one could say when confronted with such deep grief. Teng went on:

'Four years ago I had a second attack, two years later a third. The last time I was in a violent rage, and my wife had to force a soporific down my throat to prevent a terrible accident. Her unfailing support was my only consolation. Then, four weeks ago, something happened that robbed me of that consolation also. For thereafter I could no longer share my sorrow with her. The lacquer screen took possession of me.'

The magistrate paused and pointed at the high, red-lacquered screen behind Judge Dee's back. He turned and looked. The flickering light of the candles threw weird flashes on its delicately carved surface.

Magistrate Teng closed his eyes. 'Rise and observe that screen!' he said in an even voice. 'I'll describe it to you. I know it by heart, every square inch of it!'

The judge got up and walked over to the screen. It consisted of four panels, each bearing a beautifully executed

58

picture, engraved in the red lacquer, and with small fragments of green jade, mother-of-pearl, silver and gold incrusted in its surface. It was a valuable antique; he estimated that it was at least two hundred years old. He remained standing there, listening to the now nearly impersonal voice behind him.

'The four panels of the screen symbolize, as is often the case, the four seasons.* The scene on the first panel, on the left, denotes spring. A spring dream of a student, fallen asleep over his reading, on the porch of his house, in the shadow of a pine tree. While his page is preparing the tea, he dreams of four girls. They are all beautiful, but only one has caught his fancy.

'The second panel depicts summer, the season when ambitions ripen. The student has now become a full-grown man. He is travelling to the capital to pass his final examination and become an official. He rides along, followed by his page.

'Then comes autumn, on the third panel. The season of fulfilment. He has passed the final examination, and has been appointed a ranking official. Clad in Court-dress, he passes a house in his chariot, followed by an attendant who carries the large fan indicating his high office. On the balcony he sees the four girls of his dream, and among them the one he hoped to make his bride.'

The magistrate fell silent. Judge Dee went to stand in front of the fourth panel, and examined it curiously.

'The fourth panel,' Teng resumed, 'is winter, the season of introspection, of quiet enjoyment, in ever deeper understanding, of what has been acquired. It depicts the delights of matrimonial bliss.'

Judge Dee looked at the loving couple, sitting behind a table in the luxurious surroundings of an official mansion.

* *The four panels are depicted on the end-papers of this book.*

59

They were sitting very close together, the man with one arm round the woman's shoulders, and with the other raising a cup to her lips. He turned round to resume his seat, but the magistrate said quickly:

'Wait! I found this screen in a curio-shop in the capital, shortly after my marriage to Silver Lotus. I immediately purchased it, although I had to pawn some of my possessions to be able to pay the elevated price. For you must know that the four panels of this screen happen to represent the four decisive stages of my own life. When I was a student in my native place I did dream once of four girls. I did afterwards travel to the capital, and there I did see those same four girls of my dream, while passing a two-storeyed building in a chariot. It proved to be the residence of the retired Prefect Woo. And I did marry his second daughter, Silver Lotus— the girl I had singled out already in my dream! This screen was our most precious possession, we always took it with us, wherever we went. How many times we have sat together in front of it, tracing every detail, and talking about our courtship and our marriage!

'One month ago, on an exceptionally hot afternoon, I had my steward place a bamboo couch here in my library, in front of the screen, where there was a cool breeze. The pillow faced the fourth panel, the loving couple was right in front of my eyes. Then I made a frightful discovery. The design had changed. The man was plunging a dagger in his wife's breast.'

With an exclamation of surprise Judge Dee stooped and scrutinized that part of the picture. He now saw that indeed the man held a dagger in the left hand with which he embraced his wife, a dagger pointed at her heart. It consisted of a thin sliver of silver inlaid in the lacquer. Shaking his head in wonderment he went back to the table and sat down.

'I do not know,' the magistrate continued, 'when that

change occurred. Frantically I studied that particular spot, thinking that perhaps the craftsman who made the screen had accidentally dropped a sliver of silver in the still wet lacquer, and that it had come to light in that ominous place when the surface peeled off. But I soon saw that the sliver had been added afterwards, and rather clumsily, for there were tiny bursts in the area directly surrounding it.'

Judge Dee nodded slowly. He too had noticed that.

'Therefore the only possible conclusion was that I, in a fit of insanity which I didn't even remember, had effected that change. And as obvious was the second conclusion, namely that the diseased part of my mind was planning to murder my wife.'

Magistrate Teng passed his hand over his face. He looked a moment at the screen, then quickly averted his gaze. He said in a strangled voice:

'That screen became an obsession. During the last weeks I dreamt several times that I was killing my wife—horrible, stifling nightmares from which I awoke bathed in perspiration. The thought persecuted and tortured me every waking moment; the screen began to haunt me. . . . And I could not bring myself to tell this to my wife. She could bear with everything, but not that I, her husband, would ever turn against her—even if in a deranged state of mind. I knew that that would break her heart.'

The magistrate stared in front of him with unseeing eyes. Then he suddenly took hold of himself and continued in a matter-of-fact voice:

'Today we took our noon meal together outside, in a shadowy corner of the garden. But I found the air oppressive, I felt restive and thought a headache was coming on. I told my wife I would spend the siesta in my library, going over some official documents. But in my library it was also very hot, I couldn't concentrate my thoughts. Thus I decided to

61

take my siesta in my wife's bedroom.' He rose and added:
'Come with me, I'll show you.'

He took one of the candles, and they left the library together. Teng led the judge through a winding corridor to a small passage. He opened the door and, from the threshold, showed Judge Dee his wife's dressing-room. On the right stood a large toilet-table of carved rosewood with a round mirror of polished silver. On the left, in front of a narrow door, a low bamboo couch. In the centre of the floor of shining red marble tiles was a small round table of ebony, intricately carved. 'On that table,' Magistrate Teng said, 'stood the antique vase that I broke. The door on the left there gives onto a miniature garden with a goldfish pond. My wife's chambermaid always sleeps on that bamboo couch in front of it. The large, red-lacquered door you see opposite leads to my wife's bedroom. Wait here, please.'

He went inside, took an intricate key from his bosom and opened the red door. He left it standing ajar, then came back to the judge.

'When, this afternoon, I entered this dressing-room, the chambermaid was lying asleep on the bamboo couch. The last thing I remember is that I saw, through the bedroom door, which was standing ajar just as it is now, part of the bed, with my wife lying on it, naked. She was slumbering peacefully, lying half on her back, her head cradled in her folded right arm. I saw her beautiful profile, but she had laid her right leg over her left, so that the lower half of her body was turned away from me. She had loosened the long tresses she was so proud of, they provided a black-silk mat for her shoulders, then cascaded down from the edge of the bedstead. Then, just when I was about to go to her and wake her up, suddenly everything went black.

'I came to myself lying on the floor here in the dressing-room, among the broken pieces of the antique vase. My eyes

MAGISTRATE TENG DISCOVERS HIS WIFE

were blurred, I had a splitting headache, and was completely confused. I looked at the chambermaid. She was still fast asleep. I scrambled up, and stumbled to the bedroom. I remember feeling relieved at seeing that my wife was still asleep, lying exactly as I had seen her before. My attack had passed unnoticed, thank Heaven! But when I had gone inside I suddenly saw what I had done. My antique dagger was stuck in her breast, and she was dead.'

He buried his face in his hands and started to sob softly, leaning against the door-jamb.

Judge Dee quickly went into the bedroom. He surveyed the broad couch covered with a mat of closely-woven, soft reed. Near the pillow there were a few small bloodstains. Then he looked up, and saw on the wall next to the window the empty sheath of a dagger, suspended by a silken cord. By its side hung a fine old sword in a copper-studded scabbard, and a seven-stringed lute. The only window, consisting of bamboo lattice-work pasted over with thick white paper, was closed by a cross-bar of carved wood. The only other furniture was a small tea-table, a beautifully carved antique specimen of sandalwood, and two stools of the same material. In a corner stood a pile of four clothes-boxes of red leather, one for each season, richly decorated with gilded flower-motifs.

When he had rejoined the magistrate, he asked softly:

'What did you do after that?'

'That second, fearful shock completely unnerved me. I ran outside, locked the door behind me, and somehow or other succeeded in getting back to my library. While I was still trying to grasp the awful truth, feeling ill and confused, the steward came and announced your visit.'

'I am very, very sorry that my visit came at that terrible moment!' Judge Dee said contritely. 'But of course I had no idea that . . .'

'I humbly apologize for the abrupt manner in which I received you,' Magistrate Teng said formally. 'Shall we go back to my library?'

When they were seated again at the tea-table, Teng said:

'After you had left I recovered somewhat, and the routine of the afternoon session had a calming influence. There was a rather curious case of a suicide which helped to draw my mind away from the fearful tragedy. At the same time, however, I realized the legal consequences. Justice must take its course. I would have to travel to the Prefecture without delay, and give myself up to the Prefect as the murderer of my wife. But what was I to do with my poor wife's dead body, what was I to say to the steward, to the servants? Then I realized how fortunate I was in having you here, a wise and sympathetic colleague. I ordered the headman to go to the hostel I had recommended to you, and to ask you to come and see me. When he returned with the message that you had left for no one knew where, a sudden panic seized me. I had counted so much on your coming, and now you would perhaps return only the next day, or perhaps some mishap had befallen you . . . and I would have to face everything alone. Soon the servants would want to clean and air the bedroom, the steward would ask for the key. . . . I became obsessed with the idea that the dead body had to disappear. When the servants were taking their evening meal, I went to the bedroom, quickly bound up the hair, and wrapped the body in a coat I took at random. Then I carried it through the emergency exit to the back street. It was quite deserted, I reached the ruins unnoticed, and deposited my pitifully light burden in the marsh.

'After I had come back, however, I suddenly realized how foolish I had been. In my agitation I had stupidly overlooked the most obvious means for deferring the discovery of my deed, namely to pretend that I had mislaid my key of the bedroom. This was indeed the pretext I gave the steward when, after the evening-meal, he again asked me for the key. This experience convinced me that my state of mind made me wholly incapable of managing my affairs. I again sent the headman to your hostel, this time leaving an urgent message to come as soon as you returned. I waited here for you, hoping against hope that you would come, despite the late hour. And, thank Heaven, you came! Now tell me, Dee, what should I do?'

For a long time the judge made no reply. He sat there silently, staring at the screen while slowly stroking his long beard. At last he looked at the magistrate and said:

'My answer to your question is: nothing. At least for the time being.'

'What do you mean by that?' Teng exclaimed, sitting up in his chair. 'We must go to Pien-foo, first thing tomorrow morning. Let's now write a letter to the Prefect, to be sent this very night by a special messenger so that . . .'

Judge Dee raised his hand.

'Calm yourself!' he said. 'I examined the body, I saw the scene of the tragedy, and I am not satisfied that we know all the facts. I want proof that you killed your wife.'

Magistrate Teng jumped up. Agitatedly pacing the floor he shouted:

'You talk nonsense, Dee! Proof? What more proof do you want? My attacks, my dreams, that screen there . . .'

'Yet there are some very curious features,' Judge Dee interrupted him, 'features that hint at an outside element.'

The magistrate stamped his foot on the floor.

'Don't try to fool me with idle hope, Dee, that's cruel! Do you mean to make the preposterous suggestion that, just while I had my attack, an intruder murdered my wife? How could there ever be such an improbable coincidence?'

Judge Dee shrugged his shoulders.

'I don't like coincidences either, Teng. Yet such things have happened. And it is not more improbable than your having an attack and tampering with that screen, without remembering anything about it. Also, when you saw your wife upon entering the dressing-room she was lying with her back turned towards you. She may have been dead already. Have you any enemy here, Teng?'

'Of course not!' the magistrate replied angrily. 'Besides, only my wife and I knew the special significance of the screen. And it hasn't been out of the house since we arrived here. No one could have tampered with it!' Then he took hold of himself and asked in a calmer voice: 'What do you propose to do, Dee?'

'I propose,' the judge replied, 'that you give me tomorrow —one day—for gathering additional evidence. If I fail, I shall accompany you the day after tomorrow to Pien-foo, and explain everything to the Prefect.'

'Delaying the report of a murder is a grave offence, Dee!' Magistrate Teng cried out. 'Just now you said yourself you wouldn't impede . . .'

'I assume full responsibility for that!' Judge Dee interrupted him.

Teng thought for a while, nervously walking round. Then he halted and said resigned:

'All right, Dee. I'll leave everything in your hands. Tell me what I should do.'

'Very little. First, take an envelope and inscribe it with your wife's name and address.'

Teng unlocked the upper drawer of his desk and took out an envelope. After he had jotted down a few lines, he gave it to the judge, who put it in his sleeve. Judge Dee resumed:

'Now get me a set of your wife's clothes from her bedroom, and make a bundle of them. Don't forget a pair of shoes!'

The magistrate gave him a curious look, then left the room without another word.

Judge Dee quickly got up and took from the still open drawer a few sheets of official notepaper and envelopes bearing the large red seal of the tribunal. He put them carefully in his sleeve.

When Teng came in with a bundle wrapped up in blue cloth, he gave the judge a searching look, then exclaimed contritely:

'Excuse me please, Dee! I was so preoccupied by my own problems that I didn't even think of offering you a change! Your robe is dirty all over, and your boots are covered with mud. Allow me to lend you . . .'

'Don't bother!' Judge Dee interrupted quickly. 'I have a few other calls to make, in places where a new dress would attract undesirable attention. First I'll go back to the marsh now, clothe the body and drag it across the path so that it'll be found early tomorrow morning. The envelope I'll put in the sleeve, so that the body will be identified immediately. Then you'll have the autopsy conducted—you have a good coroner, I suppose?'

'Yes, he is the owner of the large pharmacy at the market.'

'Good. You'll say that your wife was murdered on her way to the north gate, and that the investigation is in progress. Then you can have the body placed in a temporary coffin at least.' He picked up the bundle, laid his hand on Teng's shoulder and said with an affectionate smile: 'Try to get some sleep, Teng! You'll hear from me tomorrow. Don't bother to show me out, I know the way.'

Judge Dee found the Student in a pitiful state. He was sitting huddled up on the boulder, with violent shivers shaking his body, despite the heat. Looking up at the judge with a sickly smile he tried to speak, but his teeth started clattering as soon as he opened his mouth.

'Don't worry, master-criminal!' Judge Dee said. 'I am back! I'll just have another look at the corpse. Then we'll be off to home and to bed!'

The youngster was so upset that he didn't notice the bundle Judge Dee was carrying.

After he had drawn out the dagger he wrapped it up in a piece of oil-paper and put it in his bosom. Then he dressed the dead body. When he had put on the shoes also, he dragged it across the footpath. He called the Student. Silently they walked back through the now deserted city.

The Student seemed still deeply upset by his lonely wait. The judge reflected that the youngster's show of viciousness was perhaps for the greater part bravado. He was only about eighteen, perhaps his morbid craving for crime would leave him in a year or so. The boy could have done worse things than join the Corporal's gang. The Corporal was a rough-and-ready rascal, but somehow or other the judge didn't think he was a really depraved man. If the Student came through this experience, he might yet repent and return to a normal life.

When they had gone about half-way, the Student suddenly said:

'I know that you and the Corporal don't think much of me, but I tell you that in a couple of days you'll be surprised! I'll have made more money than the two of you'll ever have in your whole lives!'

Judge Dee made no response. The youngster was boring him with his boasting.

At the entrance of the alley where the Phoenix Inn was located the Student halted. He said crossly:

'I'll say goodbye here. I have other things to attend to.'

Judge Dee walked on to the inn.

VII

After Judge Dee and the Student left the Phoenix Inn for the marsh, Chiao Tai drank a few cups with the Corporal. They came to talk about the battles of the Imperial Army in recent years, which evidently was one of the Corporal's favourite subjects.

'If you liked army life,' Chiao Tai asked, 'why did you leave?'

'I made a stupid mistake, and I had to take to my heels in a hurry!' the Corporal replied gruffly.

Small groups of beggars in smelly rags came drifting in. The Corporal got up and started on the accounts together with the bald man. Chiao Tai found the air in the taproom becoming worse and worse. Moreover, he was afraid that the beggar who had sold him the jewels might show up. He went out for a walk.

In the street outside it was still hot and muggy. Thinking that it might be better downtown near the river, he entered at random a sloping street. After a few wrong turns he finally arrived at the broad, curved bridge over the river. He went to stand on its highest point, leaning his elbows on the carved marble balustrade. Underneath the black water rushed along in a continuous roar, white foam spurting up as it dashed against the rocks that showed their jagged heads here and there. Chiao Tai followed the angry current as it formed swift whirlpools, and inhaled the cool air with relief.

There weren't many people about. This was evidently a residential quarter; on the right bank he saw the large compounds of opulent mansions, and on the left the long crenellated wall and the impressive gatehouse of the garrison headquarters. The coloured flags hung down limply in the still air.

Two footpads walked up to him, noiseless on their felt shoes. But when they had come nearer they shook their heads at each other disconsolately. This rough-looking giant was not the man for them to tackle.

Chiao Tai was at a loss what to do. He tried to figure out what Judge Dee was up to, but soon gave up in disgust. All that was far beyond him. And he knew that the judge would tell him anyway—in his own good time. He spat into the water, the acrid taste of the wine he had drunk in the Phoenix Inn was still in his mouth. He wistfully thought of his comrades, Sergeant Hoong and Ma Joong, back in Penglai. Probably they were at this very moment swilling good wine in the Nine Flowers Orchard, their favourite inn, on the corner opposite the tribunal! If Ma Joong was not playing games with a nice girl! He could do with a woman himself, for that matter. But he was rather fastidious, he didn't feel like having a look at a brothel. With a sigh he decided to walk back to the inn. The beggars might have left by now.

He went down the bridge and followed the river-bank for a while. At one moment he again thought he had the eery feeling that someone was following him. But this wasn't possible, because Kun-shan was now their ally. He turned into a side street which led south.

There his attention was drawn by the open window of a large house, standing back from the street behind a bamboo fence. Raising himself on tiptoe he looked over the fence, curious to see who was still up and about at that late hour. He saw a corner of a richly furnished room, brilliantly lit by two silver candles on a dressing-table. A woman clad only in a single dress of thin white silk was standing before the mirror, combing her hair.

Since of course no decent woman would thus expose herself, Chiao Tai deduced that she was a courtesan who had her own establishment. He eyed her with approval. She was a well-developed woman of about thirty, with a handsome oval face. She seemed the mature, knowing type that always appealed to him. Pensively pulling at his short moustache, he reflected again that he could do with a really nice woman, he was in the right mood for it. On the other hand, this was a high-class courtesan, and, if she would grant him her favours at all, there still was the problem of money. He had only two strings of coppers in his sleeve, and he estimated that he would need at least five, if not a silver piece. However, he could at least make her acquaintance, and maybe make an appointment for the next evening. It was worth trying anyway.

He pushed the bamboo gate open, crossed the small but elegant flower garden, and knocked on the plain, black-lacquered door. It was opened by the woman herself. She uttered an astonished cry, then quickly covered her mouth with her sleeve, looking very confused.

Chiao Tai made a bow and said politely:

'I am sorry to disturb you so late at night, younger sister! Passing by I happened to see you doing your hair by the window, and was deeply impressed by your charm. I wondered whether a lonely traveller might not rest awhile here and profit by your conversation.'

The woman hesitated. She looked him up and down, a slight frown creasing her white forehead. Suddenly she smiled and said in a soft, cultured voice:

'I was expecting someone else. . . . But, since it is long past the appointed time, you might as well come in.'

'I wouldn't dream of interfering with other appointments, I'll come back tomorrow!' Chiao Tai said hastily. 'Your guest might yet turn up—he'd be a fool if he didn't!'

CHIAO TAI WATCHES A CHARMING LADY

The woman laughed. He thought she was really very attractive.

'Do come in!' she said. 'I rather like your looks, you know!'

She stepped back, and Chiao Tai followed her inside.

'Sit down,' she said coyly, 'I'll just fix my hair.'

Seated on a tabouret of coloured porcelain, Chiao Tai reflected ruefully that he would be lucky if he could persuade her to make an appointment for some other night, for this was clearly a courtesan of the most expensive class. A thick blue carpet covered the floor, the walls were decorated with heavy brocade hangings, and the broad couch was made of blackwood inlaid with small figures of mother of pearl. The fragrant smoke of some expensive incense curled up from the gilded burner on the dressing-table. He twirled his moustache, looking with appreciation at her shapely back and rounded hips. He followed for a while the graceful movement of her white arm as she combed her long, glossy tresses. Then he said:

'I am sure that a lovely lady like you has a charming name!'

'My name?' she asked, smiling at him in the round mirror. 'Oh, you may call me Autumn Rose.'

'It sounds well,' he said, 'but of course no name could ever do justice to your exquisite beauty!'

She turned round with a pleased smile and sat down on the edge of the couch. Taking a fan from the side table she leisurely fanned herself, looking at him appraisingly. After a while she said:

'You are strong and not too bad-looking, though a bit austere. And your robe is plain though of good material, but you don't know how to wear it to advantage. Shall I guess what you are? I think you are an army officer on leave!'

'Very near!' Chiao Tai said. 'And it is indeed true, as I told you just now, that I am a stranger in town.'

She looked at him intently with her large, luminous eyes. Then she asked:

'Do you plan to stay long in Wei-ping?'

'I have only a few days. Now I have met you, I wish I could live here for ever!'

She playfully tapped his knee with the fan and asked:

'Does the army teach its officers such nice things nowadays?' She gave him a sidelong look and carelessly let her robe come apart in front, revealing her perfect breasts. 'Oh, isn't it hot, even at night!'

Chiao Tai shifted on his tabouret. Why didn't the old duenna appear with the customary tea? Since the courtesan had clearly indicated that he was acceptable, according to the etiquette of the 'world of wind and willows', he could now discuss the price with her duenna. She looked at him expectantly. Chiao Tai cleared his throat, then asked awkwardly:

'Where could I find your eh . . . duenna?'

'Why would you want my duenna?' she asked with lifted eyebrows.

'Well, I wanted to talk with her a bit, you know . . .'

'Talk with her? What about? Don't you like my conversation?'

'Stop your teasing!' Chiao Tai said with a smile. 'About . . . the practical aspects, of course!'

'Now, what on earth would you mean by that?' she asked, pouting.

'Holy Heaven!' Chiao Tai exclaimed impatiently. 'We are neither of us children any more, are we? There's the matter of how much I am expected to pay, how long I can stay, and so on.'

She burst out laughing, covering her mouth with her fan.

Chiao Tai joined her, rather embarrassed. When she had recovered, she said primly:

'I regret to inform you that my duenna is ill. So you'll have to discuss the "practical aspects", as you so delicately put it, directly with me. Well, speak up, sir, at how much do you value my favour?'

'Ten thousand gold pieces!' Chiao Tai replied gallantly.

'You are a dear!' she said gratified. 'And a strong animal to boot. You lead your wives at home quite a strenuous life, I am sure. Well, today is a special day. You can stay with me for a while and we shall forget about those hateful practical aspects of yours. It so happens that I'll be leaving town shortly, and a second visit from you would not be convenient. So you must promise that after tonight you'll not come back here again.'

'You break my heart, but I promise!' Chiao Tai said. He envied the wealthy patron who would be taking this delightful woman along on a trip. He rose, and sitting down by her side he put his arm round her shoulders. While giving her a long kiss he began to loosen the sash of her robe.

VIII

Chiao Tai walked to the Phoenix Inn, humming a tune. He found the taproom deserted but for Carnation, looking sullen. She was sweeping the floor with a bamboo broom. She asked:

'Where is the Student?'

'Around!' he replied, letting himself down carefully in the old rattan armchair, the easiest he saw about. 'Make a large pot of tea, will you? Not for me, but for my mate, he's a great tea-bibber! Didn't Kun-shan come?'

Carnation made a face.

'He did, that mean bastard! I told him both of you were out, and he said he would be coming back later. I can tell you that I have put up with all kinds of men, but with that Kun-shan I wouldn't sleep for ten gold pieces!'

'You can always keep your eyes shut, can't you?' Chiao Tai asked.

'No, it isn't his ugly mug. He's the vicious kind that likes to hurt. I might find myself with my throat slit, and what do I do then with ten gold pieces?'

'Use them for bribing the Black Judge of the Nether World! But let's not talk about Kun-shan. What about me, dear, eh?'

The girl stepped up to him and gave him a good look. She sniffed contemptuously.

'You? Next week perhaps, when you've recovered! That smug smirk of yours tells me that you just got as thorough a treatment as you'll ever be likely to get. And expensive too, judging by that smell! No, I wager that you haven't even the strength left to lift my skirt!' She went to the kitchen.

Chiao Tai guffawed. He leaned back in the chair, put his feet on the table and soon was snoring loudly. The girl came back and put a large teapot on the table. Then she yawned, walked over to the counter, and started to pick her teeth.

It was she who opened the door for Judge Dee. She asked anxiously: 'Why hasn't the Student come back with you?'

The judge shot her a shrewd look, then replied:

'I sent him out on another job.'

'He won't get himself into trouble, will he?'

'Nothing I can't get him out of. You look tired, my wench. Better go up to sleep. We'll be here for some time.'

She went up the narrow staircase, and Judge Dee woke Chiao Tai.

Chiao Tai's face fell when he saw how haggard and tired the judge looked. He quickly offered him a cup of hot tea and asked anxiously: 'What happened?'

Judge Dee told him about the dead body, and his conversation with Magistrate Teng. He hadn't quite finished when there came a soft knock on the door. Chiao Tai went to open it and found himself face to face with Kun-shan. 'Holy Heaven!' he grunted. 'There's that ugly snout again!'

'You might at least say thank you!' Kun-shan remarked coldly. 'Good evening, Mr Shen! I trust you find your new quarters comfortable?'

'Sit down!' Judge Dee said. 'I admit that you did us a good turn. Now explain the reason!'

'To tell you the truth,' Kun-shan replied, 'I don't care a tinker's curse whether they catch you and your mate and chop off your heads on the execution ground. But I happen to need you, and I need you in a hurry. Listen! I am the most skilful and most experienced burglar in this province,

78

I have been at this job more than thirty years and I have never once been caught. However, I lack bodily strength, and I've never tried to acquire it either, because I think violence is vulgar. Now I happen to have a job in mind that probably will need a dose of violence for its successful completion. I've observed you two carefully, and I think you'll do. Much to my disgust, I'll have to let you share in the profit. Since I did all the difficult preliminary work, and since the risk involved is insignificant, I take it that you'll be satisfied with a very modest amount.'

'Plainly put,' Chiao Tai interrupted. 'We'll have to do the dangerous work and you'll walk off with the prize. Modest share, you say? It'll cost you plenty, you dirty coward!'

At the last word Kun-shan's face grew pale, it had evidently touched a raw spot. He said venomously:

'It's easy to play the hero when you are strong! And you think you are quite a man with the ladies too, don't you? Tonight I thought that solid couch would collapse under your capers! As the poet says: "The torrential rain crushes the autumn rose".'

Chiao Tai jumped up, gripped Kun-shan by his neck and threw him on the floor. Placing his knee on his breast and encircling his throat with his large hands, he growled:

'You dirty swine, you spied on me! I'll break your neck for that!'

Judge Dee quickly leaned over and grabbed Chiao Tai's shoulder. 'Let him go!' he said sharply. 'I want to hear his proposal!'

Chiao Tai rose and let Kun-shan's head fall on the floor with a dull thud. He lay still, his breath rattling in his bruised throat.

Chiao Tai's face was livid with rage. He sat down heavily and said curtly:

'Tonight I was with a courtesan. This rat spied on us.'

'Well,' Judge Dee said coldly, 'I would have thought that you'd manage your amorous affairs more discreetly. Anyway, I won't have them interfere with my investigation. Douse the rascal's head!'

Chiao Tai went over to the counter. He took the large basin of washing-up water, and threw it over Kun-shan's head. 'It'll take some time before the son of a dog wakes up,' he muttered.

'Sit down! I'll tell you the rest about Teng,' the judge said impatiently.

By the time Judge Dee had finished his account of the lacquer screen, Chiao Tai's anger had passed. He said eagerly:

'What an astounding story, Magistrate!'

Judge Dee nodded.

'I didn't feel like telling my colleague my strongest reason for suspecting that an outsider had killed his wife. And that is that I found she had been raped. I didn't wish to distress the poor fellow further.'

'But didn't you say that her face looked peaceful?' Chiao Tai asked. 'I can't say I have any experience in raping a sleeping woman, but I suppose she'd wake up and make it known that she was annoyed, wouldn't she?'

'That is only one of the many puzzling aspects of this strange case,' Judge Dee said. 'Be careful! I think Kun-shan is coming to!'

Chiao Tai dragged the ugly man up and made him sit down in the rattan chair. Kun-shan swallowed with difficulty. He groped for the teacup and drank slowly. Then he croaked at Chiao Tai: 'I'll make you pay for that, bastard!'

'Present the bill any time you like!' Chiao Tai said.

Kun-shan fixed him with a malicious glare from his one eye. He sneered:

'You don't even know the merry widow pulled your leg, you fool!'

80

'Widow?' Chiao Tai shouted.

'Certainly a widow, and a brand-new one too! You came to the side door of the residence of the late Ko Chih-yuan, you blockhead, the silk merchant who killed himself only yesterday! His widow had moved from the common bedroom to her small boudoir in the left wing, in order to nurse her grief in solitude. But you, experienced ladies' man, stupidly mistook her for a courtesan!'

Chiao Tai's face went scarlet with shame and mortification. He wanted to speak, but managed only some unintelligible sounds. Judge Dee took pity on him and said quickly:

'Well, perhaps his wife's morals had something to do with Ko's suicide.'

Kun-shan tenderly felt his throat. He gulped down a cup of tea, then said nastily:

'Women have no morals, and Mrs Ko is no exception. However, my business with you concerns the merchant Ko too, strangely enough. Listen to me carefully, I'll be brief. There came into my hands a notebook belonging to Leng Chien, a well-known banker of this city who was Ko Chih-yuan's associate and financial adviser. I am versed in financial matters, and I soon saw that the notebook contained Leng Chien's secret records of how he has been swindling old Ko during the past two years by faking accounts. He made a considerable amount of money that way, about one thousand gold, I would say.'

'How did you get that notebook?' Judge Dee asked. 'It isn't the kind of record a banker would leave lying about!'

'None of your business!' Kun-shan snapped. 'Now look here, I . . .'

'Wait a moment!' the judge interrupted him. 'I too happen to be interested in financial matters—that's why I had to leave my post as headman in a bit of a hurry. You must be a real wizard to be able to derive all that information

81

from annotations on complicated financial transactions, and secret too! You had better think up a more probable story, my friend!'

Kun-shan gave the judge a suspicious look.

'You are a cunning scoundrel, aren't you? Well, since you insist on knowing the ins and outs, let me tell you that I have visited Ko's residence a few times—without him knowing it, of course. I have examined the contents of his safe and found there an emergency fund of two hundred gold pieces— which is now my emergency fund—and also his papers, which I studied with considerable interest. Those papers gave me the background for Leng Chien's notebook, so to speak.'

'I see,' Judge Dee said. 'Proceed!'

Kun-shan took from his sleeve a small sheet of paper, which he carefully smoothed out on the table. Tapping it with his spidery forefinger, he resumed:

'This is a page I tore from the notebook. You two will visit our friend Leng Chien tomorrow morning, show him this page, and tell him that you know everything. You'll ask him to write out two drafts, one for six hundred and fifty gold pieces, and the other for fifty, leaving the name of the payee blank. That little blood-letting will leave him with three hundred in gold—which is not to be sneezed at. I would much prefer to take the whole lot, but the secret of successful blackmail is that you give your man an out, so as not to make him desperate. The draft of six hundred and fifty you give to me. You two keep the one of fifty. Fifty good pieces of gold. Is it a deal?'

Judge Dee fixed the ugly man with his piercing eyes, leisurely caressing his side-whiskers. Then he said slowly:

'My mate here put it a bit bluntly, Kun-shan, but he hit the nail on the head. I fully believe that you are a past master in stealing and breaking in, but you lack the courage for a man-to-man encounter. You know very well you could never in your life muster the courage to face that banker and blackmail him, could you?'

Kun-shan shifted uneasily in his chair. 'Is it a deal or not?' he asked surlily. The judge took the sheet of notepaper and put it in his sleeve.

'It is,' he said, 'but share and share alike. Remember that, with the paper you so kindly gave me, I don't need you and your notebook for blackmailing Leng Chien. Why shouldn't I keep all the money for myself?'

'Why indeed!' Chiao Tai said with a pleased grin.

'And why shouldn't I report to the tribunal where they can find two highway robbers?' Kun-shan asked nastily.

'Because you wouldn't dare, that's why!' Judge Dee replied calmly. 'Make up your mind!'

Kun-shan gave him a vicious look. He put his hand to his cheek, trying to suppress its nervous twitching. At last he said:

'All right then, share and share alike.'

'That's settled!' the judge said with a satisfied air. 'I'll visit our friend Leng Chien first thing tomorrow morning. Where can I find him?'

Kun-shan explained the location of Leng Chien's silver shop, where Leng also conducted his banking business. Then he rose to leave. But Judge Dee put his hand on his arm and said affably:

'The night is still young! Let's have a cup of wine together and drink to our partnership!' And, to Chiao Tai: 'Search behind the counter for the Corporal's special jug!'

Chiao Tai left the table, wondering why the judge, utterly tired as he was, wanted to prolong the conversation with that unspeakable cad. He found the waiter fast asleep on the second shelf of the counter, and on the third the Corporal's jar, which he brought over to their table.

When they had emptied a cup, Judge Dee wiped off his moustache and said:

'You may be a master-thief, Kun-shan, but that's child's play compared to our work. Let me tell you a few adventures we've had on the road. You remember, mate, that time in Kiangsu Province, when we . . .'

'I am not interested in your tall tales!' Kun-shan interrupted him sourly. 'Your work is based on brute force, mine on brains! It takes years and years to become a real expert at burglary.'

'Nonsense!' Judge Dee shouted. 'Even I can manage to open a door lock from the outside! Once you are in the house, you overpower the owner, ask him politely where his valuables are, take them, and off you go! There's nothing to it!'

'It's you who are talking nonsense!' Kun-shan said angrily. 'Your method is that of the common, stupid robber. He gets away with it once or twice, but then the hue and cry is out for him and he is caught. I have my own method, which I have practised for more than thirty years. And I've never been caught once, despite the fact that I usually work in the same city for a couple of years.'

The judge gave Chiao Tai a broad wink.

'He is a glib talker, isn't he?' he asked. 'He has a secret method, you know, transmitted only from master to pupil, on the ninth day of the waning moon!'

'Since you two are nothing but a couple of vulgar rowdies,' Kun-shan said with scorn, 'there's no harm in telling you. You could never in your life even start to imitate me! This is how I work. I begin by studying the house, its inmates and all their habits for a few weeks. I talk to the servants, I talk to the shopkeepers in that neighbourhood, I invest a bit of money in these inquiries. Then I break in, but I don't take anything, I have plenty of time, you see. I just have a look around the house. I can stay in a cupboard for hours on end, stand concealed in the fold of a curtain, curl myself up in a clothes-box, or squeeze into the narrow space behind a bedstead. Thus I observe the people who live there waking and sleeping, I listen to their most intimate conversations, I spy on them when they think they are alone. Then, at last, I make my final visit. There's no forcing of locks, no frantic searching. Nobody is disturbed, nothing is displaced. If there is a secret hiding-place for the money, I know it better than its owner; if there is a safe, I know exactly where to find the keys. Nobody ever sees or hears me. Often it takes them days to realize that their money is gone! And then they don't think of a burglar! No, husbands begin by suspecting wives, wives suspect concubines. . . . I fear I have caused numerous misunderstandings and brought discord to many a harmonious household!' He chuckled, covering his mouth with his hand. Then he concluded in a harsh voice: 'Well, my clever friend, now you know my method!'

'Remarkable!' Judge Dee exclaimed. 'I hate to admit it, but I could never do that. I don't doubt that your secret observations have taught you a thing or two about men and women, including a few new tricks on the bedmat, eh?'

Kun-shan's face contorted in a grimace that made him look even more repulsive. He hissed:

'Spare me your smutty jokes! I hate and despise women and the dirty games their loathsome men play with them. I hate those hours I must spend hidden in bedrooms, hearing lewd creatures cooing to their stupid husband while selling him their bodies, or coyly feigning to refuse him till he is cringing and wheedling for what I see them offer gratis to their lovers. Those sickening, abominable . . .' He suddenly checked himself. Sweat was pearling on his brow. Glaring at

85

the judge with his one eye, he got up. He said in a hoarse voice: 'I'll meet you here at noon tomorrow.'

As soon as the door had closed behind him Chiao Tai exclaimed disgustedly:

'What a foul creature! Why in the name of Heaven did you want to listen to his ranting?'

'Because,' Judge Dee said calmly, 'I hoped to hear from him about methods for breaking-in that might indicate how an intruder entered Mrs Teng's quarters. Second, I wanted to learn a little more about Kun-shan's character, and I got quite an instructive lesson on how frustration can warp a man's mind.'

'Why his sudden love for us?' Chiao Tai asked sourly.

'Presumably because we are exactly the combination he needs for his blackmail scheme. He knows that I, who look fairly respectable, I trust, can gain admittance to the banker's private office, and am capable of conducting the negotiation, while he trusts you to add physical pressure, if that should prove necessary. Moreover, we are strangers here. He couldn't easily find a pair of crooks so eminently suited to his purpose, and I presume that that's why he went out of his way to contact us. However, there's still the possibility of a snake in the grass somewhere. I didn't like his quick acceptance of my proposal to share the loot. I had expected long and complicated bargaining. Well, anyway, we'll have to see to it that Kun-shan is put behind bars, and for the rest of his life. He is an evil, dangerous villain.' The judge passed his hand over his eyes, then went on: 'I'll now write a note to the coroner. Try to find me an ink-stone and writing-brush. I suppose the Corporal needs them, if only for jotting down his dots and crosses!'

Chiao Tai rummaged behind the counter. He brought out a dirty, broken ink-slab and a worn-down brush. Judge Dee burned off the brush's superfluous hairs in the candle and, by dint of much licking, succeeded in giving it a sharp point. Then he took from his sleeve the official notepaper and envelope he had abstracted from Magistrate Teng's desk, and wrote in an impersonal, official hand:

To the Coroner. You are instructed to proceed without delay to Four Goats Village, where your presence is urgently required for an autopsy.

Teng, Magistrate of Wei-ping

He gave the letter to Chiao Tai, saying:

'I don't want the coroner to conduct an autopsy on Mrs Teng's corpse. There is no need to distress my unfortunate colleague further by letting him know that his wife was raped. Deliver this letter early tomorrow morning to the owner of the large pharmacy on the market place, you'll easily find it. We passed Four Goats Village on our way from the Prefecture. It is a five-hour ride, so that'll keep the coroner out of the way tomorrow.' He scratched his head with the end of the writing-brush, then continued: 'Since I am making such liberal use of Teng's permission to act on his behalf, I might as well write another note borrowing his name!' He took a new sheet of official paper and wrote:

To the Officer in charge of Personnel, Garrison Headquarters. Urgent. You are requested to have the files searched for data on a certain Liu, a deserter who in recent years served as Corporal in the Third Wing of the Western Army. Hand the pertinent extract to the bearer of the present.

Teng, Magistrate of Wei-ping

Handing it to Chiao Tai, he said:

You can take this note to the Garrison Headquarters some time tomorrow. I expect we'll have to avail ourselves of the Corporal's hospitality for a few days and, as the proverb says, "Don't stay in another's house unless you know the host well." Let's go upstairs and inspect our quarters! '

IX

Judge Dee spent a most uncomfortable night. The doghole assigned to him and Chiao Tai was barely large enough for two narrow plank-beds. The judge had lain down as he was, but his robes did not protect him long against the hordes of voracious vermin that instantly opened their attack. He hardly slept at all. Chiao Tai had found a better solution. He just stretched himself out on the floor between the beds, with his head to the door, and soon had joined the snoring orchestra that reverberated through the thin wooden partitions of the other rooms.

They got up soon after dawn and went downstairs. There was no one yet in the taproom. The inmates of the Phoenix Inn evidently did not believe in early hours. Chiao Tai rekindled the kitchen stove and they made a perfunctory toilet. When Chiao Tai had prepared a pot of hot tea for the judge, he went off to deliver the letter to the coroner. Judge Dee sat down at the corner table, and sipped his tea.

Carnation came down, woke up the waiter by thumping the counter hard with her fist, and then went to the kitchen to prepare the morning gruel. Soon afterwards the Corporal and his four assistants also made their appearance. The Corporal drew up a chair to Judge Dee's table, but indignantly refused a cup of tea. He shouted at Carnation to warm a bowl of wine for him. When he had drunk that with evident satisfaction, he asked:

'How did it fare last night, brother?'

'The dead woman must have been a wealthy lady,' the judge replied. 'And the fellow who did it was rich too, for he left these baubles on her.' He took the earrings and the bracelets from his sleeve and laid them on the table. 'When I have disposed of these, you'll get half the proceeds.'

'Heaven!' the Corporal said admiringly, 'that was well worth a trip to the marsh, eh? She was surely murdered by a man of her own sort; you must have a fat purse to let such good stuff go! Keep on trying to find the bastard, you might blackmail him. And tell him at the same time that, if he has other women to kill, I'd thank him for doing the job outside my city.'

A ragged vagabond came in and asked for a free bowl of gruel. When he had greedily gobbled it down, standing at the counter, he called out to the Corporal:

'Have you heard the news, boss? They've just brought the dead body of the magistrate's wife to the tribunal. She's been murdered in the marsh.'

The Corporal hit his fist on the table and cursed violently.

'You were damn well right when you called her a lady!' he shouted at the judge. 'You'd better find that murderer quick, brother! Bleed him for as much as you can, then bring him to the tribunal. Hell and Heaven—the magistrate's wife, of all people!'

'Why the excitement?' Judge Dee asked astonished.

'You know what an Imperial official is, don't you? If your or my wife gets her throat cut and we report it, the constables just beat us up and say that we should look after our household goods better. But the wife of a magistrate, brother, that's something else! If the fellow who did it isn't found plenty quick, this whole town'll be crawling with military police, secret police, special agents from the Prefecture, special investigators and their men, and all the other vermin that call themselves the law. They'll comb the city, brother, and make arrests left and right. You and me'll have to pack up in a hurry and leave! That's why I am excited, brother, and that's why I tell you: set to work and get the bastard!'

He stared moodily at his wine-cup. Judge Dee said:

'It won't be so easy though, seeing that the fellow was a member of her own class.'

'He was her sweetheart, of course!' the Corporal growled. 'Those so-called gentlewomen! The knots of their trouser-cords are tied as loosely as those of our own jades! The fellow got tired of her, she made a fuss, and he bashed her head in. Old story! Well, I'll call my men together, and let them have a look at these baubles. They'll ferret out where the slut used to play her games with our magistrate's belly-cousin. That'll help you to trace the son of a dog.'

'That's a good idea,' the judge said, just to humour his host. Suddenly he looked up from his gruel and asked curiously: 'How would your men go about that? None of them will even know her by sight!'

'They'll know her baubles, won't they?' the Corporal asked impatiently. 'It's their job! When you or me see an expensive skirt go by, either on foot or carried in a litter, we try to get a peep at her muzzle. But a beggar looks only at the trinkets she carries. He has been trained to do that, it's his rice-bowl! If he sees a valuable earring behind a veil, or a nice bracelet on the hand that moves the curtain of a palankeen, he appraises its value, and, if it's good stuff, he knows it'll be worth while to follow that woman. She may let drop an expensive handkerchief, or even a few coins. Now these baubles are high-class workmanship and made to order, so there's a good chance that one of my men noticed them. Do you get it now?'

Judge Dee nodded. He pushed the jewels over to the Corporal, reflecting that he was picking up interesting knowledge that might come in useful on a future occasion. He saw Chiao Tai coming in and said to his host:

'I'll be off now to look after a little affair of mine. I'll be back presently.'

While the two men were walking towards the market place, Chiao Tai asked:

'I suppose now we go straight to your colleague Teng with the story of that banker's malversations?'

'Not so fast!' the judge replied. 'First we go to visit Leng Chien, and verify the truth of Kun-shan's story by blackmailing the banker.'

As the dumbfounded Chiao Tai made no response, Judge Dee continued:

'If Leng Chien lets himself be blackmailed, it means that he confesses that he has been guilty of fraud. We must reckon with the possibility, however, that Kun-shan is playing us some nasty trick. I'll observe the banker's reactions. If I think we can go ahead, I'll give you a sign.'

Chiao Tai nodded. He hoped for the best.

Leng Chien's silver shop presented an impressive front. It occupied a large, two-storeyed building on a busy corner of the market place. The shop front was open to the street, and had a counter more than twenty feet long. Behind it a dozen clerks were busy serving a crowd of customers, weighing silver, appraising jewels, exchanging coppers for silver and vice versa. Above the babble of voices one heard the monotonous singsong of two cashiers who were checking accounts.

Judge Dee walked over to the chief clerk, who was sitting at the end of the counter behind a high desk, busily clicking the beads of his abacus. He pushed his visiting-card under the wooden grille and said politely:

'I would like to speak to Mr Leng personally, if possible. I wish to transfer a sum of money. It's rather a large amount.'

The clerk looked doubtfully at the two tall men, and asked some questions about the deal they were engaged in. Judge Dee told a plausible story about a speculation on the rice market. The clerk, reassured by his cultured language, jotted down a few words on his card. Then he shouted to an office boy to take the card upstairs. After a while the boy came back with the message that Mr Leng would see Mr Shen and his associate.

The banker, clad in a neat white mourning-dress, was seated at a large red-lacquered table. While busily talking to two clerks he pointed to two high-backed chairs at the tea-table in front of the window, and one of the clerks quickly poured out tea for the visitors. Judge Dee looked at the banker while he was giving his final instructions to the two clerks. He thought the man was looking pale and worried. Then he surveyed the room. He was struck by a scroll hanging on the wall behind the banker, a large painting of lotus flowers, accompanied by a long poem written in an expressive hand. From where he was sitting he could just make out the signature: 'Your ignorant younger brother, Te.' Evidently this was Leng Chien's brother Leng Te, the young painter who had died two weeks before, as the spectator in the tribunal had told him.

Leng sent the clerks away. Turning to his guests, he asked briskly what he could do for them.

'It concerns the partial transfer of about one thousand in gold, Mr Leng,' Judge Dee said evenly. 'This is the most important document pertaining to the transaction.'

He took the notebook page out of his sleeve, and placed it on the table.

Leng's face turned ashen. He stared aghast at the piece of paper. Judge Dee felt relieved. He nodded to Chiao Tai. The big fellow stood up and ponderously walked to the door, which he bolted. Then he stepped up to the window and pulled the shutters closed. The banker followed his movements, panic in his eyes. As Chiao Tai went to stand behind the banker's chair, Judge Dee continued:

'I have, of course, the rest of the papers too. Quite a bulky notebook.'

'How did you get it?' Leng asked tensely.

'Come now, Mr Leng!' the judge said reprovingly. 'Let's not digress, shall we? I am not an unreasonable man, you know, but, as you have seen from my visiting-card, I am a commission agent, and I expect of course my commission on your profit. I calculate that you made about one thousand gold pieces.'

'How much do you want?' the banker asked in a strained voice.

'Only seven hundred,' Judge Dee replied calmly. 'That'll leave you a nice capital to start working with again.'

'I ought to denounce you to the tribunal!' Leng muttered.

'And I ought to denounce *you*!' the judge said affably. 'So let's call it quits.'

Suddenly Leng buried his face in his hands. He wailed:

'It's Heaven's retribution! Ko's ghost is persecuting me!'

There was a knock on the door. Leng Chien wanted to jump up, but Chiao Tai laid his heavy hands on his shoulders and pressed him down again, whispering hoarsely into his ear:

'Don't get excited now, please! That'd ruin your health! Tell them to go away!'

'Come back later! I can't be disturbed now!' the banker called out obediently.

Judge Dee had been studying him, slowly caressing his sidewhiskers. Now he asked:

'Since Ko didn't know about your cheating him, why worry about his ghost?'

The banker gave the judge a startled look.

'What are you saying?' he panted. 'Tell me, was the envelope open or closed?'

The judge had not the faintest idea what the agitated

banker was talking about. He had taken it more or less for granted that Kun-shan had stolen the notebook when robbing Leng Chien's house. But apparently it was much more complicated than that. He said pensively:

'Let me see now, I did not particularly notice. . . .' He reflected that the notebook had evidently been placed in an envelope. It seemed probable that it had been sealed. He added: 'Yes, I remember now! The envelope was closed.'

'Heaven be praised!' Leng exclaimed. 'Then I didn't send him to his death!'

'Now you have said so much, you'd better tell the entire story!' Judge Dee commented dryly. 'I told you already that I am a reasonable man, I might be willing to talk over the deal.'

Leng wiped the sweat from his forehead. Evidently it was a relief to be able to tell someone now about his secret worries. He said:

'I made a stupid mistake. When Ko had invited me to dinner, he asked me to bring along for him a bundle of documents which he wanted to check. I placed them in an envelope, sealed it, and put it in my bosom. But when I arrived at Ko's place, I forgot to give him that envelope. When we were half-way through the dinner, just before Ko became ill, he asked me about it. I put my hand in my bosom and by mistake took out the sealed envelope containing my notebook, which I always carried about with me and which was the same size and weight as the one with the business papers. I handed that envelope to Ko, and realized my terrible mistake only after Ko had gone back to the house to take his medicine. When I saw him throw himself into the river, I assumed of course that he had opened the envelope in his bedroom, discovered that I, his best friend, had been deceiving him, and committed suicide

95

in despair. That terrible thought has been obsessing me all through these last two days. I couldn't sleep at night, I . . .'

He shook his head disconsolately.

'Well, you can't complain that you aren't getting your money's worth from us!' Judge Dee said. 'I suppose you were planning to sneak out of the city one of these days?'

'I was,' Leng Chien replied. 'If Ko hadn't died, I would have fled this week, leaving a letter for him in which I explained everything, and begged him to forgive me. I needed nine hundred gold pieces for paying my debts, and planned to use the rest for starting anew in a far-away place. After Ko died, I hoped to get the tribunal to register his demise quickly. Then I would have had access to his safe, where I know he keeps two hundred gold pieces. But now I'll have to leave as soon as possible. My debtors will have to do without their money.'

'I won't keep you much longer,' the judge said. 'Our business is quite simple. Where did you deposit the gold?'

'With the Heavenly Rain gold shop.'

'Good!' Judge Dee said. 'Make out two drafts of three hundred and fifty gold pieces each and addressed to that shop. Sign and seal them, but leave the name of the payee blank.'

Leng took from a drawer in his desk two large sheets, covered with the seals of his silver shop. He groped for his writing-brush and filled them out. The judge took them and saw that they were in order. Putting the sheets in his sleeve, he said: 'May I borrow that nice writing-brush for a moment, and a sheet of paper?'

He turned his chair so that the banker could not see what he was writing. Chiao Tai remained standing behind Leng's chair.

Judge Dee spread the paper out on the tea-table and jotted down a brief message in his own, expressive handwriting:

To Kan, the elder brother. I beg you to send your men to Leng Chien's silver shop immediately and arrest the banker on the charge of fraud. This case is connected with Ko Chih-yuan's demise. I shall explain later.

The younger brother Dee Jen-djieh bows twice

He put the sheet in an envelope of the shop, and sealed it with the small personal seal he always carried with him. He rose and spoke:

'I'll say goodbye now, Mr Leng! You'll not leave this shop for one hour. My assistant here'll watch from the other side of the street. It would be unhealthy for you to try to leave earlier. Perhaps we'll meet again!'

Chiao Tai unlocked the door, and the two men went downstairs.

When they were in the street Judge Dee handed Chiao Tai his note to Magistrate Teng. Adding one of 'Mr Shen's' visiting-cards, he said:

'Run as fast as you can to the tribunal, and see that the magistrate gets this letter immediately! I am going back to the Phoenix Inn.'

X

When the judge entered the taproom he found the Corporal standing at the counter, talking to an old man clad in a tattered robe. The waiter was pouring out a cup of wine for them. Carnation sat cross-legged on a stool near by, paring her toenails.

'Come here, brother!' the Corporal shouted. 'I have good news for you. Hear what this fellow has to say!'

The old man gave the judge a baleful look from watering, red eyes. He had a thin, weather-beaten face, as wrinkled as the skin of a crab-apple. Pulling at his ragged, greasy beard, he began in a whining voice:

'My regular stand is on the corner of the second street on the left side of the west gate. The fourth building there is a closed bawdy house, but of class, you see. I have a good, steady income there.'

'It's a nice place,' Carnation remarked, 'I've been taken there once or twice, when my luck was in.'

The beggar turned round to her and gave her a bleary look.

'I saw you!' he said sourly. 'Next time you'd better tell your customer to give me more than two coppers! Tell him I expect at least four. Sometimes I even get more, if the gentleman comes out with a pleased mug!'

'Come to the point!' the Corporal snapped.

'Well, the jade wearing the earrings you showed me went there two times. I couldn't see her face because she wore a veil, but I did see those earrings peeping out from under. When she comes out with the young fellow, she looks at me and says to him, "Give the poor man ten coppers." Which he did.'

'You needn't look so astonished,' the Corporal said to Judge Dee. 'Those beggars make good money, you know! You should try it yourself, some day!'

The judge managed to mutter something. This was a totally unexpected development. Barring the most unlikely eventuality—that there existed a second pair of those earrings in Wei-ping—Mrs Teng must have had a secret lover, which was not only unlikely, but wholly unthinkable! He asked the beggar sharply: 'Are you quite sure she was actually wearing those same earrings?'

'Look here, you!' the old man said indignantly. 'My eyes may run a little bit now and then, and then only on really windy days, but I'll wager they're better than yours, see!'

'Drip-eye knows his job,' the Corporal said impatiently. 'Now you go to work on that young man, brother. That's your murderer! What did he look like, Drip-eye?'

'Oh, just a well-dressed youngster. Bit of a tippler, I'd say, for he had red patches on his cheeks. Never seen him anywhere else.'

Judge Dee slowly stroked his beard. He said to the Corporal:

'I'd better be off and question the people in that house.'

The Corporal guffawed. He poked the judge in the ribs and said:

'You think you're still a headman, eh? Arrest the people, put them on the rack, and they'll tell you everything! What do you think the madame would do when you went there asking questions? Offer you a turn, on the house?'

The judge bit his lip. Things were moving too fast, he was making bad mistakes. The Corporal went on seriously:

'The only way to learn something there is to go with Carnation and rent a room, businesslike! Those people know her, so nobody'll get suspicious. If you can't trace your murderer, then you'll at least learn something from the wench. She knows her job, eh, Carnation? And gratis too!'

'You'll have to invest a few strings of coppers,' the girl said listlessly. 'It's not a cheap place. And, as for me being gratis, we'll have to see about that. Here at home I go with the room, but outside work is different.'

'Don't worry about that,' the judge said. 'When can we go there?'

'After the noon meal,' she replied. 'Those places don't open earlier than that.'

Judge Dee offered a cup of wine to the Corporal and the beggar. The latter set out on a long tale about some of the queer things he had seen in his career. Presently Chiao Tai came back and joined them. They had a few rounds together, then Carnation went to the kitchen to prepare the noon rice. The judge said to Chiao Tai:

'This afternoon I am taking her to a nice house near the west gate.'

'I thought you had better things to do than to go whoring!' an unpleasant voice spoke up behind them. Kun-shan had come in noiselessly on his felt shoes.

'I settled the affair we talked about,' Judge Dee told him. 'Come on, we'll take you to a restaurant. We feel we owe you a meal!'

Kun-shan nodded and the three men left the inn together.

In the next street they found a small eating-house. Judge Dee took a table somewhat apart from the others and ordered a large platter of fried rice and pork, salted vegetables and three jars of wine. As soon as the waiter had left, Kun-shan asked eagerly:

'Did Leng Chien pay up? We'll have to hurry, for they have just arrested him, I hear.'

Silently Judge Dee took the two drafts from his sleeve and

KUN-SHAN ANGRILY LEAVES THE RESTAURANT

displayed them. Kun-shan put out his hand with a suppressed cry of delight. But the judge quickly put the papers back in his sleeve. He said coldly:

'Not so fast, my friend!'

'Are you going back on our bargain?' Kun-shan asked threateningly.

'You cheated us, Kun-shan!' Judge Dee snapped. 'You made it seem that it was just a matter of milking a crooked financier. You forgot to tell us that there is a murder linked up with this affair!'

'Nonsense!' Kun-shan hissed. 'What murder?'

'The so-called suicide of Mr Ko Chih-yuan!'

'I know nothing about that!' Kun-shan said angrily.

'You'd better tell the truth, bastard!' Chiao Tai barked. 'We don't like to be made scapegoats!'

Kun-shan opened his mouth, but checked himself when he saw the waiter approaching with the food and wine. When he had gone, Kun-shan snarled:

'It's nothing but a dirty trick! Give me that draft, I tell you!'

Judge Dee had taken up his chopsticks. He filled his bowl, took a few mouthfuls, then said calmly:

'You give me that notebook, and you tell me exactly how and where you got it. Then you'll get your draft, not before.'

Kun-shan jumped up, overturning his chair. Livid with rage, he shouted:

'You'll hear from me, you dirty crook!'

Chiao Tai grabbed his arm and pulled him back. 'Let's take him to the inn,' he said to the judge, 'and have a quiet talk with him, upstairs!'

Kun-shan wrenched himself loose, cursing obscenely. Bending over to the judge, he hissed: 'You'll regret this!'

Chiao Tai wanted to rise, but Judge Dee said quickly:

'Let him go! We can't have a brawl here!' And, to

Kun-shan: 'You know where to find us, and how to get your money!'

'I certainly do!' Kun-shan snapped. He turned round and left.

'Is it wise to let that scoundrel go?' Chiao Tai asked dubiously.

'When he has calmed down,' the judge said, 'he'll remember his money and turn up again.' Looking at the heaped-up platter of rice and the three wine-jars on their table, he added: 'But what shall we do with all that?'

'That's the least of your worries, magistrate!' Chiao Tai said with a grin. He took up his chopsticks and fell to with gusto. The fried rice diminished with amazing speed.

Judge Dee did not feel hungry. Absent-mindedly turning his wine-cup round in his hand, he reflected that the news about Mrs Teng's secret meetings had taken him so completely by surprise that he would have to be careful not to let himself be rushed into hurried action. He had made a bad blunder at the inn, and now he also began to doubt whether he had dealt with Kun-shan in the right manner. The man was dangerous, and he knew very little about him, not even where his regular hide-out was. He began to wonder uneasily whether he had taken on too much.

Judge Dee had drunk only one cup of wine, but Chiao Tai took care of the rest. Smacking his lips, he said:

'Superior quality! Now, what work is there for me this afternoon?'

Wiping off his beard and moustache with the hot towel, the judge said:

'Go to the Garrison Headquarters and try to get that information on the Corporal. I don't think he is involved in any of our problems, but I have learned one can apparently take nothing for granted here! Then you might pay a visit to the soothsayer Pien Hoong, the man who warned Ko

Chih-yuan that on the fifteenth his life would be in danger. Find out whether he is a genuine soothsayer or a charlatan, and also whether he knows Kun-shan. At the same time you might make him gossip a bit about Ko. That merchant's death is a mystery that greatly intrigues me.'

He paid the bill, and they strolled back to the Phoenix Inn.

XI

Carnation was waiting for the judge. She had changed into a dark-blue robe and a black silk jacket. With her hair done up in a simple chignon she did not look unattractive, despite her vulgar make-up.

There was no one else in the taproom. She said that the others had gone upstairs for their afternoon nap.

'I'll follow their example, for a while,' Chiao Tai said. 'That wine was rather heady! But I prefer to take my siesta down here.'

He let himself down heavily into the old rattan armchair. Judge Dee and Carnation went out into the hot street.

The girl walked a few paces ahead of the judge, as was customary for a prostitute taking a client with her. If a man went out with his wife she would, on the contrary, walk a few paces behind him.

Carnation knew many short-cuts. Soon they entered a quiet street lined with prosperous-looking, middle-class houses. It seemed a quarter of retired shopkeepers. She halted before a high door, neatly lacquered black. Nothing indicated that it was a house of assignation.

Judge Dee knocked, but when a portly lady dressed in black damask opened, it was Carnation who spoke first and asked for a room. This indicated that it had been she who suggested the address to the customer, and thus was entitled to a commission.

Smiling, the madame let them into a small sitting-room. She said they could have the best room for the afternoon, on payment of three strings of coppers. The judge protested and, after long haggling, they agreed on two strings. The judge paid and she took them upstairs to a large and richly furnished bedroom. After she had left, Carnation said:

'This really is the best room in the house. You can be sure that the lady used this one for meeting her lover.'

'We shall search it!' Judge Dee said.

'You'll have to wait a bit. Soon the woman'll be coming back with the tea. Don't forget to give her a small tip then, it's the custom.' Seeing that Judge Dee was going to sit down at the tea-table, she said casually: 'I don't know what you have in mind, but anyway we'd better change into bedrobes. The people here have sharp eyes. They'll get suspicious if we don't act like other guests.'

She went to the dressing-table, took off her jacket and her robe and stepped out of her wide trousers. Judge Dee disrobed also, and put on the clean bed-robe of white gauze that was hanging ready on the lacquered clothes-rack next to the bedstead. Carnation was standing naked in front of the dressing-table, washing herself with the unconcern of members of her trade. It struck the judge that she had a shapely body. When she bent over, his eye fell on the thin white scars that ran criss-cross over her back and hips.

'Who has been maltreating you?' he asked angrily. 'The Corporal?'

'Oh no,' she said indifferently. 'It's already more than a year ago. I wasn't sold to the brothel as a child, you know. I was sixteen already, and I didn't like the work, so I got a whipping now and then. But I was lucky. One day the Corporal came along and took a fancy to me. He told my owner that he wanted to buy me out. The man showed him the receipt for forty silver pieces that my father had signed when he sold me.' She turned round and put on the bed-robe. Fastening the silk sash, she continued with a smile: 'My owner was just starting to count up the other expenses that would have to be refunded, when the Corporal grabbed the paper from him and said: "All right, the deal is closed!" When my owner asked about the money, the Corporal just glared at him and said: "I just paid you, didn't I? Or would you call me a liar?" You should have seen the fellow's sour face! But he produced a smile and stammered, "Yes, sir, thank you, sir!" and the Corporal took me along. My owner knew that, if he complained to his guild or to the tribunal, the Corporal would come with his men and smash all his furniture. I certainly was lucky. The Corporal may be a bit short-tempered, but he's a good fellow at heart. And I don't mind those scars, they are my badge of trade, so to speak!'

While listening to her the judge had been pulling out the drawers of the dressing-table. 'There's nothing here,' he said, 'absolutely nothing.'

'What did you expect?' the girl asked, sitting down on the edge of the bedstead. 'Everybody who comes here takes good care to leave nothing that might show their identity. They know that these houses are not averse to a bit of black-mail, at times. Your best chance is the inscriptions and pictures put up inside the bedstead here. They are signed only with pen-names, I've always heard, but, since you can read, you might find something there.'

The woman came in with a large tray, loaded with a tea-pot and platters of fresh fruit and candy. Judge Dee gave her a handful of coppers, and she left with a polite smirk.

Carnation drew the curtains aside and entered the bed-stead. Judge Dee took off his cap and placed it on the tea-table. Then he stepped up into the large bedstead also, and sat down cross-legged on the spotless reed-mat. The bedstead was a small room in itself. Its back and side walls were made of carved blackwood, the panelling reaching high up to the canopy. Carnation was kneeling in front of the back wall, carefully forcing a hair-needle into a fissure of the wood.

'What are you doing there?' the judge asked curiously.

'I jammed the door of the secret peephole,' she replied. 'I don't think there'll be customers for it this early in the day, but you never know. And anyway we don't want them to discover what we're up to.'

She sat down opposite the judge and leaned back against the large pillow.

Judge Dee reflected that he certainly was picking up much useful knowledge. Before his marriage to his First Lady he had occasionally associated with the high-class courtesans of the capital, but he was ignorant of the customs of common houses of prostitution, and the depraved tastes they catered for. He raised his head and, caressing his side-whiskers, began to study one by one the sheets inscribed with poems and pictures that had been inserted into the many square and round frames in the panelling. The bedsteads of married couples are usually decorated with inscriptions and pictures of an edifying kind, alluding to the deep meaning of the married state, and to virtuous men and women of antiquity. Here, however, they were of course of a more frivolous nature. Literary people who visit houses of assignation and brothels often amuse themselves by jotting down a few impromptu verses or making a few sketches. If those are cleverly done, the management will use them for decorating the inside of the bed. When they have faded, they are torn down and replaced by new ones. The judge read aloud a couplet, written in a flowing, scholarly hand:

'*Beware lest the same Gate through which you entered life,*
Becomes the Gate through which you meet untimely death.'

He nodded and said:

'Crudely expressed, but unfortunately quite true.' Then he suddenly sat up. His eye had fallen on a poem of four lines. The first couplet was written in the same unconventional, artistic hand as the inscription on the painting of the lotus flowers which he had seen in Leng Chien's office, on the wall behind the banker's chair. The second couplet was written in the very small, precise calligraphy taught to girls of good family. There was no signature. He slowly read out aloud the first couplet:

'How fast the days and nights flow past, a river swift
  and unremitting,
  Carrying too few and too frail fallen blossoms in its
  hasty stream.'

And then the second couplet, which ran:

'Let them flow by, don't stay them, their petals'll wither
  in your hand,
  However tender. You'll spoil them for another loving
  couple's dream.'

According to the old poetic custom, the man had written down a couplet, and the woman had capped it with a second. It would seem to fit. The poem with its allusions to fallen blossoms and short-lived earthly pleasures could well refer to an illicit relationship. The beggar had described Mrs Teng's lover as a well-dressed young man with red cheeks. Those red patches need not have been caused by indulging in wine, they could be the tell-tale signs of the lingering lung disease Leng Te had died from. And the young painter's predilection for depicting lotus flowers would seem to supply further proof. He said to Carnation: 'This poem could have been written by Mrs Teng and her lover together.'

'I don't quite get the meaning,' the girl said, 'but it sounds to me like a sad poem. Did you recognize her lover's handwriting?'

'I think so. But, even if I am right, it won't help us much in finding Mrs Teng's murderer. The young man who wrote the first couplet is dead.' He thought for a while, then went on: 'You'd better go downstairs now and try to get that woman to give you a good description of the couple.'

'You're very anxious to get rid of me, aren't you?' the girl said curtly. 'You'll have to bear with my company a little longer, though. We must keep up appearances.'

'I am sorry!' Judge Dee said with an apologetic smile. He had not thought that the girl was so sensitive. And she was quite right, of course. 'I am a bit preoccupied,' he added quickly, 'but I like your company very much. How about bringing that tea-tray here? Then we can eat and drink a little, and talk some more.'

Carnation silently climbed down from the bedstead and fetched the tray. When she had placed it on the bedmat between them, she poured out two cups of tea. She ate a piece of candy. Suddenly she said:

'It must be a nice change for you to be in a real bed again, like the one you have at home.'

'What is that?' the judge asked, startled from his thoughts. 'At home? You know very well that men of my profession have no home!'

'Oh, stop that nonsense!' Carnation exclaimed, annoyed. 'You act the part fairly well, so you needn't fear that the Corporal or his men'll find you out. But don't think you can fool an experienced woman when you are in bed with her!'

'What do you mean?' Judge Dee asked, irritated.

She leaned over and pulled his robe down. Quickly feeling his shoulder, she said contemptuously:

'Look at that smooth skin! A daily bath, and expensive

ointments! And do you want me to believe that your hair got that gloss from the wind and rain? You are strong, but your skin is white and without a single scar. Those muscles of yours you got from fencing and boxing in the training-hall, with the other young gentlemen! And the cheap way you're treating me! You may think I am not worth a second look, but let me tell you that no real highwayman or vagrant crook would be sitting calmly on the bedmat with me here, daintily sipping his tea! Those men get a chance at a woman like me only once in a while; even if they were on a job they'd grab me as soon as I had lowered my trousers, and worry about the job afterwards! They can't afford to be as casual as you, with your four or five fawning wives and concubines at home who coddle you day and night, and who have expensive powder instead of stripes on their behinds! I don't know who or what you are, and I care less, but I won't be insulted by you and your haughty airs!'

Judge Dee was taken aback by this sudden outburst. He did not quite know what to say. The girl went on in a bitter voice:

'Since you don't belong to us, why come and spy on us? Why spy on the Corporal, a fine fellow who trusts you completely? To laugh and joke about us later when you're back with your own people, I suppose?'

Angry tears had come into her eyes.

'You are right,' the judge said quietly, 'I am indeed act-ing a part. But certainly not as a cheap joke. I am an official engaged in a criminal investigation, and you and the Cor-poral, without knowing it, are giving me exactly the assis-tance I had been hoping for when I assumed my role. As to me not belonging to you, there you are completely wrong. I have sworn to serve the state and the people, and that includes the Prefect's First Lady as well as you, the Prime Minister as well as your Corporal. We, the great Chinese

111

people, all belong to each other, Carnation. That is our eternal glory, and that makes us, the cultured people of the Middle Kingdom, different from the uncouth barbarians of the rest of the world, who hate and devour each other like wild beasts. Am I making myself clear? '

The girl nodded, somewhat mollified, and wiped her face with her sleeve.

'Another thing,' Judge Dee went on. 'Let me assure you that I think you are a very attractive woman, you have a sweet face and a splendid figure. If I didn't happen to have a lot of other things on my mind just now, I would be very happy indeed if you would grant me your favours! '

'It probably isn't true,' Carnation said with a thin smile, 'but it sounds nice anyway. You do look tired. Lie down and I'll fan you! '

Judge Dee stretched himself out on the soft mat. The girl let the robe slip down from her shoulders, took the palm-leaf fan that hung in a corner of the bedstead, and started to fan him. Before he knew it he was sound asleep.

When he woke up he saw Carnation standing fully dressed in front of the bed.

'You had a good nap,' she said, 'and I had a good talk downstairs. The woman paid me a decent commission, too. I'll use that for buying myself a present from you! '

'How long have I slept? ' Judge Dee asked anxiously.

'A couple of hours. The woman downstairs remarked that you must be an ardent lover. She also told me that the couple came here twice, just like old Drip-eye said. She was a slight woman, but very distinguished, quite a lady. The young man was also of good family, but he didn't seem very strong; he was suffering from a bad cough. He paid handsomely. The woman also said that both times the couple had been followed.'

'How do you mean, followed? '

JUDGE DEE AND CARNATION

'Right into this house and this room! Both times another fellow came in shortly after the couple had gone upstairs, and paid a round sum for using the peep-hole up in the bedstead there.'

'Who was that man?' the judge asked tensely.

'Did you expect him to leave his visiting-card? The woman downstairs said he was tall and thin. He had pulled his neck-cloth over his face up to his eyes, so she couldn't see what he looked like, and his voice was muffled. But she's sure he was an educated man, with a certain air of authority about him. And he walked with a limp.'

Judge Dee remained standing still, with his robe in his hands. That could have been no one else but Teng's counsellor, Pan Yoo-te! Silently he put on his robe, assisted by Carnation. When he had wound the sash round his waist and put on his cap, he felt in his sleeve and said, somewhat diffidently:

'I am deeply grateful for your excellent help. Allow me to offer you a . . .'

'The information was gratis, for nothing!' the girl interrupted him curtly. 'But I wouldn't mind your taking me here again, some other day. I am sure you could keep a girl quite agreeably occupied—when your mind isn't on other things, at least. Then you can pay me sixty coppers, and a hundred if you want to make a night of it. That's my regular price when I work outside.'

She went to the door. Downstairs the madame was waiting for them, and obsequiously escorted them to the door.

In the street the judge said to the girl:

'I'll have to go to the north quarter now. I'll see you again at the inn, at meal time.'

She gave him a few directions about the road north, then they parted.

XII

This time Judge Dee entered the tribunal by the main gate. He gave his red card, reading 'Shen Mo, Commission Agent', to one of the guards, together with a small tip, and asked him to have it brought to Counsellor Pan. Soon a clerk came and led him past the chancery to Pan Yoo-te's office.

Pan pushed a pile of official documents aside and bade Judge Dee sit down opposite him. He poured a cup of tea from the large pot on his desk, then began, with a harried look on his face:

'You'll have no doubt heard the terrible news, Mr Shen! The magistrate is nearly distracted with grief. I am really worried about him. This morning he suddenly had the banker Leng Chien arrested, you know. And Leng is one of our prominent citizens. The whole town is talking about it! I do hope that the magistrate didn't make a mistake. . . . Everything goes wrong today! There couldn't be an autopsy, as our coroner had left town without even informing us! And the man is always so punctilious!' He suddenly remembered his manners and asked quickly: 'I trust you had a pleasant day, Mr Shen? Did you visit the Temple of the City God? It was rather hot this afternoon, I fear, but I hope——'

'I did visit a very curious place,' the judge cut him short, 'in the second street to the left of the west gate.'

He closely watched Pan's face, but it was completely blank.

'The second street?' Pan repeated. 'Oh, now I know! You've made a slight mistake. It's the third street you mean, of course! Yes, that old Buddhist chapel there is quite unusual; it's very old, you know. It was founded three hundred years ago by an Indian priest who . . .'

Judge Dee let him tell the entire story without interrupting him. He thought that, if it had been Pan who had spied on the couple, he certainly was a consummate actor. When Pan had concluded his historical dissertation, the judge said:

'I mustn't take too much of your time. Mrs Teng's murder is keeping you very busy, of course. Is there any clue to the murderer yet?'

'Not that I know of,' Pan replied. 'But then the magistrate may know more. He keeps the investigation entirely in his own hands, quite understandably, of course, seeing that the victim was his own wife! A tragedy, a terrible tragedy, Mr Shen!'

'It will be very sad news for all their friends,' Judge Dee remarked. 'Since Mrs Teng was a poetess, I assume that she belonged to some literary ladies' circle here?'

'I can see,' Pan said with a smile, 'that you don't know the Tengs very well! They went out very little, you know. The magistrate took part in all official functions, of course, but apart from that he kept very much to himself; he doesn't have any particular friend among the gentry here. He takes the view that a magistrate ought to be completely impartial and have no local attachments. And Mrs Teng hardly went out at all. She only used to spend a few days regularly with her widowed sister. The husband was a wealthy landowner; he died young, when he was thirty-five and she just thirty. He left her that splendid country house outside the north gate. The air there did Mrs Teng a lot of good. The maids said she always looked so cheerful and well when she came back from there. And she needed it this time too, for the last couple of weeks she had been in bad health and looked very pale and sad. . . . And now she is dead!'

After a suitable pause Judge Dee decided he would try another direct attack. He said casually:

'Today I happened to see in a shop a painting by one of the local artists, called Leng Te. They said he knew Mrs Teng well.'

Old Pan looked astonished for a moment. But then he said:

'I didn't know that, but it's very likely, now I come to think of it. The painter was a distant relative of the dead landowner, he also visited the country house of Mrs Teng's elder sister frequently. Yes, he must have met Mrs Teng there, of course. A pity he died so young, for he was a gifted artist. His pictures of birds and flowers were excellent. He specialized in lotus flowers, in quite an original style, too.'

The judge thought that this was getting him nowhere at all. He had learned where the lovers could have met, but he hadn't come one step nearer to the main issue, the identity of the mysterious third person involved. And the madame's description seemed to point directly at Pan: tall but thin, the air of authority, the limp. . . . He decided to make a last attempt. Leaning forward, he said in a low, confidential voice:

'Yesterday you told me much about the historical sites of this city, Mr Pan. Now those are very interesting for daytime. But after dark the thoughts of a lonely traveller naturally turn to, ah . . . more recent art, more tangible beauty, one might say. Doubtless there are a few places here where charming damsels . . .'

'I have neither the inclination nor the leisure for frivolous entertainment,' Pan interrupted him stiffly. 'Hence I am unable to give you any information on that particular subject.' Then, remembering that, after all, this vulgar fellow had come with an introduction from the Prefect, he added with a forced smile: 'I married rather young, you see,

117

and I have two wives, eight sons and four daughters.'

Judge Dee reflected ruefully that this truly impressive record definitely disposed of the possibility that old Pan was a pervert. The mysterious visitor had to be another person, as yet unknown. Perhaps Mrs Teng's writings would supply a clue. He emptied his teacup, then resumed:

'Although as a simple merchant I don't claim to understand much of literature, I always read the magistrate's poetry with great admiration. I never saw, however, an edition of his wife's collected poems. Could you tell me where I could find one?'

Pan pursed his lips.

'That's difficult!' he replied. 'Mrs Teng was a woman of a most sensitive disposition, and of extreme modesty. The magistrate told me that he had often tried to persuade her to have her work published, but she always resolutely refused, so that he had to give up in despair.'

'That's a pity,' Judge Dee said, 'I would have liked to read her poetry, to enable me to say a few sympathetic things to the magistrate about it, when I go to offer him my condolences.'

'Well,' Pan said, 'perhaps I can help you. Last week Mrs Teng sent me a copy-book containing her poems, written out by herself. She added a note asking me to verify whether there were mistakes in some references to the historical sites of Wei-ping. I'll have to return the manuscript to the magistrate soon, but if you want, you can have a look at it now.'

'Excellent!' Judge Dee exclaimed. 'I'll just sit down with it over by the window there, so that you can get on with your work!'

Pan opened a drawer and took out a bulky volume bound in plain blue paper. The judge went over to the armchair in front of the window.

First he quickly leafed through the volume. It was written in the same neat hand as the second couplet of the poem he had seen in the house of assignation, with only some minor differences. These could, of course, be explained by the fact that the copy-book had been written out carefully in the quiet library, while the couplet was jotted down during a secret rendezvous.

Then he began to read the poems, from the beginning. Soon he found himself completely captivated by this truly magnificent poetry. Judge Dee took the narrow Confucianist view that the only poetry worthy of the name served either an ethical or didactic purpose. In his youth he himself had written a long poem on the importance of agriculture. He had little interest in verses that were just lyrical effusions or that recorded only fleeting moods. But he had to admit that Mrs Teng's masterful command of the language and her original imagery lent her poetry a compelling beauty. She had the gift of the adjective; as a rule she used only one to define a mood or scene, but that one word summed up all the essential features. Some of the striking similes he remembered having encountered in the magistrate's published poetry also, evidently the pair had worked together very closely.

He put the volume in his lap and sat there staring at nothing, pensively caressing his side-whiskers. Pan shot him an astonished look but the judge did not notice it. He asked himself how it could be possible that a great poetess, a refined, sensitive woman, happily married to a husband with whom she shared the same interests, could ever become an adulteress. That a woman whose delicate sentiments were so convincingly recorded in her poetry, could ever stoop to the sordidness of secret meetings in a bawdy house—the smirking madame, the sly tips—it seemed utterly incredible. A sudden, passionate affair with a rough-and-ready youngster, violent and brief—such a thing might not be wholly impossible. Women were strange creatures. But the young painter had been the same type of man as her own husband, with the same interests. He angrily tugged at his moustache. It didn't fit at all.

Suddenly he remembered the slight differences in the handwriting. Could it be that the woman who secretly met the painter was not Mrs Teng, but her elder sister, the young widow? She had worn Mrs Teng's earrings and bracelets, but sisters often lend each other their trinkets. The painter had been a distant relative, so the young widow had had even more opportunities for meeting him than had Mrs Teng. Moreover, there were two other sisters. He asked Pan:

'Tell me, are Mrs Teng's other sisters also living in the country house outside the north gate?'

'As far as I know,' Pan replied, 'there's only one sister there, Mr Shen, and that is the landowner's widow.'

The judge returned the volume to him. 'Excellent poetry!' he commented. He now felt sure that the young widow had been Leng Te's paramour. Of course her handwriting would resemble closely that of Mrs Teng. When they were still young girls they would have been taught by the same private tutor. Probably the elder sister had planned to marry the painter as soon as the years of mourning prescribed by the rites had passed. Their secret meetings were of course utterly wrong, but that was no concern of his. Neither was he interested in the depraved taste of the mysterious man who had spied on the couple. He had been wrong. He rose with a sigh and asked Pan to announce him to the magistrate.

When Judge Dee was seated with Magistrate Teng at the table in his library, he said:

'Tomorrow we'll leave here for the prefectural city, Teng.

I did my best, but I have failed to discover the slightest in-
dication that my theory about an intruder being implicated
in the death of your wife was correct. You were right, it
would indeed have been too much of a coincidence. I am
sorry, Teng. Tonight I shall try to evolve a plausible explanation for Mrs Teng's body having been found in the marsh,
and I shall take full responsibility for the delay in reporting
the tragedy to the Prefect.'

Teng nodded gravely. He said:

'I deeply appreciate all you have done for me, Dee! It is
I who must apologize for the trouble I put you to, and that
on your holiday! Your presence in itself is a great comfort
to me. Your sympathetic understanding and readiness to
help are things I shan't easily forget, Dee.'

The judge was touched. Teng would have been fully justified in showering reproaches on him, for he had tampered
with evidence and retarded a murder investigation. Moreover, he had given Teng idle hopes. It flashed through his
mind that he was glad indeed he had sent the coroner away
with a faked message. In this hot weather decomposition
would have so far advanced by now that a detailed autopsy
would be impossible. Thus Teng would fortunately never
know what he had done before killing his wife. Judge Dee
still thought it very strange, but one really knew very little
about the vagaries of a sick mind. He said:

'I hope you'll give me a chance to try to make myself useful in another respect, Teng. Namely, in the case of Ko Chih-
yuan's demise. I expect that you'll say you are sick and tired
of my theories, but the fact is that I happened to stumble
on some rather interesting ramifications of that case. The
banker Leng Chien is involved in it. He confessed to me that
he had been swindling Ko for large amounts. That is why
I sent you the message asking you to have him arrested. I
just heard that you complied with my request at once. I am

really quite embarrassed by your confidence in my slender abilities, Teng! But I trust that in this case at least I shan't disappoint you!'

The magistrate passed his hand over his eyes with a weary gesture.

'That's true!' he said, 'I had quite forgotten about that case!'

'Today you won't feel like going into that further, I suppose. You would really do me a favour if you would allow me to conduct an investigation, together with your counsellor.'

'By all means!' Teng replied. 'You are perfectly right in thinking that I couldn't give that complicated case the attention it deserves. I can't think of anything but our interview with the Prefect tomorrow. You are really very thoughtful, Dee!'

The judge felt embarrassed. Outwardly Teng might seem a cold man, but his reserve concealed a warm nature. He had been a fool to assume that his wife had been deceiving him. He said:

'Thank you, Teng! I would propose that you tell Pan my real identity, so that I can go over the official records of the case with him.'

The magistrate clapped his hands. When the old steward appeared he told him to summon Pan Yoo-te.

The old counsellor was taken aback when he learned Judge Dee's identity. He immediately started upon a long apology for his casual attitude towards him. But Judge Dee cut him short, and asked Teng to excuse them.

When the still confused Pan was leading him to his private office, the judge noticed that it had grown dark outside. He said to Pan:

'I think that both of us are entitled to a bit of fresh air! I would be pleased if you would join me for dinner in a restaurant, and order some local specialities for me.'

Pan protested that he couldn't possibly accept that honour; but the judge insisted, adding that to the outer world he was, after all, still Mr Shen, the commission agent. At last the old counsellor agreed. They left the tribunal together.

XIII

Pan had chosen a small restaurant on one of the city's many hills. From the balcony they had a magnificent view over the moonlit town.

There was fresh river fish stewed in ginger sauce, roasted snipes, smoked ham, quail-egg soup and other local specialities which tasted so good that Judge Dee felt somewhat ashamed when he thought of Chiao Tai, who, at that moment, would be gobbling the plain bean-flour gruel of the Phoenix Inn.

During the meal Pan gave a lucid summing up of the facts of Ko Chih-yuan's case. Then the judge told him about Leng Chien's malversations, about Kun-shan's stealing the notebook, and about the two hundred gold pieces which Ko kept in his safe. He vaguely hinted that it had been Kun-shan who had blackmailed the banker, but that he, the judge, had made Kun-shan hand the two drafts to him.

Then he asked:

'Does the tribunal have a file on Kun-shan?'

'No, Your Honour. I have never even heard his name! It's truly astounding! You have learned in two days more about this city than I have in all my years here.'

'I have been lucky. By the way, I heard that Mrs Ko is much younger than her husband was. Could you tell me when Ko married her, and whether there are other wives or concubines?'

'Ko originally had three wives,' Pan replied, 'but his First and Third Lady died a few years after their marriages. His Second Lady passed away one year ago. Since Ko was already over sixty then, and since his sons had grown up and his daughters had married, everybody thought that he would take a concubine to look after him, and leave it at that. However, one day he visited a small silk shop that used to purchase its stock from his firm. The owner, a certain Hsieh, had died, and his widow was trying to continue the business, but had got into debt. Old Ko fell violently in love with her, and insisted on marrying her. At first people made jokes about it, but Mrs Ko proved herself an excellent wife. She managed the household well, and when Ko began to suffer from his stomach attacks she didn't leave his bedside. So in the end everybody agreed that Ko had acted very wisely.'

'Were there ever rumours about her being unfaithful to him?' Judge Dee asked.

'Never!' Pan replied immediately. 'She has an excellent reputation. That's why I didn't dare to suggest that she be heard as witness in the tribunal. I questioned her myself in the hall of their mansion, directly after the tragedy. In the accustomed way, of course, she sitting behind a screen, and attended upon by her maidservant.'

Judge Dee thought he would like to meet Mrs Ko. Pan's praise did not tally at all with Chiao Tai's adventure. He said:

'I would like to see the scene of the tragedy. We have the entire evening before us, so let's go and pay a visit to the Ko residence. You can say that I am an official, temporarily attached to the tribunal.'

Pan nodded. He said:

'I too would like to have a second look there, especially at the bedroom. We can do that without inconveniencing Mrs Ko, for I heard that she has had their common bedroom locked, and has moved to a boudoir in an outhouse of the left wing.'

Judge Dee paid the waiter. He then suggested that they hire a sedan chair, but Pan said he could manage to walk downhill with his limp. A leisurely stroll brought them to the Ko mansion downtown.

It had a high gatehouse, and thick pillars of granite flanked the red-lacquered door, lavishly decorated with brass bosses. The steward received them in the main hall, tastefully furnished with antique chairs and tables of massive ebony. After he had offered the guests tea and fruit, he went to inform his mistress of their request. He came back with several keys. Mrs Ko had raised no objection.

The steward had a lighted lampion brought. He led them through a maze of dark corridors and courts to a small walled-in bamboo garden. At the back was a low building which, the steward explained, old Mr Ko had chosen for his private quarters since it had a broad terrace overlooking the garden and the river.

He unlocked the solid door and went in first in order to light the candle on the centre table. 'If more light is needed,' he said, 'I shall light the large oil lamp.'

Judge Dee quickly surveyed the bare, sparsely furnished room. The atmosphere was stuffy. Apparently the door and the window had not been opened in the last two days. He walked over to the narrow door in the wall opposite. The steward unlocked it for him and he descended three steps into a short passageway. When he opened the door at its end, he saw a broad marble terrace and beyond that the garden, shelving away to the river-bank. The garden pavilion where Ko had his last dinner stood more to the left, its green-glazed roof-tiles glistening in the moonlight.

He remained standing on the terrace for a while, enjoying the beautiful scene. Then he went back into the house. He noticed that the terrace door was rather low, but that only a man much taller than he would hit his head against it. When he stepped up into the bedroom again, he saw a tall woman clad in white standing against the wall on the left.

126

She was a handsome lady of about thirty, with a regular, oval face. The loose mourning-robe could not entirely conceal her well-proportioned figure. As he saw her standing there, looking very distinguished with her downcast eyes, Judge Dee said to himself that Chiao Tai had good taste, the rascal! Better than his friend and colleague Ma Joong, who had a rather unfortunate proclivity for noisy, vulgar women. He made a deep bow, and Mrs Ko responded by inclining her head.

Counsellor Pan respectfully introduced Judge Dee as Mr Shen, temporarily assigned to the tribunal on special duty. Mrs Ko raised her large, luminous eyes and gave the judge an appraising look. She turned to the steward and told him he could go. Then she motioned to the judge and Pan to sit down in the two chairs in front of the broad, low window next to the door through which they had entered. She herself remained standing, stiffly erect. As he sat down Judge Dee now noticed in the shadows next to her, a demure young maidservant. Playing with her fan of white silk, Mrs Ko addressed Pan in a cold, formal voice:

'Since you took the trouble to come here for an investigation, I thought it my duty to see personally that everything is being done to facilitate your work.'

Pan started on an elaborate apology, but Judge Dee interrupted him:

'We are deeply grateful, madam,' he said politely. 'I fully realize how painful this visit to the scene of the tragedy must be for you. I would not have caused you this distress were it not for my earnest desire to have all the formalities connected with your husband's demise over and done with as soon as possible. I sincerely hope, therefore, that you will forgive this intrusion.'

Mrs Ko made no response, she confined herself to gravely inclining her head. The judge reflected that, for a former shopkeeper's wife, she had indeed quickly acquired the manners of a well-born lady. He continued briskly:

'Now, let me orientate myself!' He casually looked at the large bedstead with plain blue curtains, drawn closed, that stood against the wall opposite Mrs Ko. Behind her he saw the usual pile of clothes-boxes of red-lacquered leather. The whitewashed walls and the stone-flagged floor were bare. He remarked in a conversational tone:

'This room seems to contain very little furniture, madam. I suppose there was more when your husband was still alive? A dressing-table, perhaps, and a few scroll pictures on the walls . . .'

'My husband,' Mrs Ko interrupted him coldly, 'was a man of frugal taste. Despite his great wealth he was averse to all luxury, and lived in an austere manner.'

Judge Dee bowed.

'That, madam, is eloquent proof of his noble character. Now, let me see, what points did I wish to verify?' His eye fell again on the clothes-boxes, and he continued: 'Look, there are only three of those boxes, marked Autumn, Winter and Spring. Now where would the fourth be, containing the summer garments?'

'I had it removed to be repaired,' Mrs Ko replied in a tired voice.

'I see,' Judge Dee said. 'It just struck me that one is missing, one is so accustomed to seeing a set of four. Now, madam, I would like you to tell me, as well as you can remember, what happened here on that fatal night. I have, of course, seen the court records, but . . .'

Suddenly Mrs Ko hit out at something with her fan. She snapped at the maid:

'How many times have I told you already that I don't want those horrid creatures in the house? Quick, hit it . . . there it goes!'

Judge Dee was astonished by this sudden vehemence. Pan Yoo-te said soothingly: 'There are only one or two, madam, shall I . . .'

Mrs Ko did not hear him. She followed intently the maid's frantic attempts to catch the fly, slapping at it with her handkerchief.

'Why don't you hit it?' Mrs Ko burst out impatiently. 'There it is . . . quick now!'

The judge had been watching her with intense interest. Suddenly he rose. He took the candle and made to light the large oil lamp that stood next to it.

'Don't light that lamp!' Mrs Ko snapped.

'Why not, madam?' Judge Dee asked meekly. 'I only wanted to help you to see whether there are more flies.' He lifted the candle and looked up at the ceiling.

'It's not respectful to have too many lights in a room of the dead!' Mrs Ko remarked coldly. But the judge did not hear her. He had been looking fixedly at the ceiling. He said slowly:

'Now, isn't it curious, madam, that there are so many flies in this room? Especially since it has been closed for two days. Look, they seem a bit drowsy up there, but the light will cheer them up!'

Ignoring Mrs Ko's protests, he quickly lit the four wicks of the oil lamp. Lifting it above his head he scrutinized the ceiling. Mrs Ko came forward and followed his gaze. She had grown pale and she was breathing heavily.

'Are you unwell, madam?' the maid inquired anxiously. But her mistress paid no attention to her. She shrank back as a swarm of flies came down and started to buzz around the lamp.

'See,' Judge Dee said to Pan, 'they are flying lower now, the light has lost its attraction for them!'

The old counsellor stared at him dumbfounded. He looked as if he thought that the magistrate had taken leave of his senses.

The judge had walked over to the bedstead. Stooping he examined the floor. As he righted himself, he exclaimed, half to Pan and half to Mrs Ko:

'Isn't that strange! They assemble here along the fringe of the bed curtain!'

He lifted the curtain and peered under the bed.

'Ah!' he said. 'I see. It's the floor they are interested in. Or rather, I suppose, something under the floor.'

He heard a suppressed cry behind him. He swung round and saw Mrs Ko fall to the floor. She had fainted. The maid quickly went to her and knelt by her side. The judge walked over to her, and looked down at her prone body for a while. Pan Yoo-te muttered worriedly: 'She has had a heart attack, we must . . .'

'Nonsense!' Judge Dee snapped at him. And, to the maid: 'Leave her alone! Come here, and help me to push the bedstead over to the other side. If you could also lend a hand, Pan—it's rather heavy, I fear.'

But the floor was so smooth that they succeeded in moving the bedstead over to the window without much difficulty. Judge Dee knelt down and examined the stone flags. He took a toothpick from his lapel and probed in the grooves. Then he stood up. He said to Pan: 'Some of these slabs have been taken up recently!' Turning to the maid, he barked: 'Run along and bring me a kitchen knife and a shovel. And don't start gossiping with the other servants! Come back here immediately, do you hear?'

After the frightened maid had scurried away, Judge Dee looked gravely at Pan and said: 'A devilish scheme!'

'Yes, sir!' Pan replied. His dazed look showed that he had not the faintest idea what the judge was talking about.

JUDGE DEE AND PAN YOO-TE IN MR KO'S BEDROOM

However, Judge Dee did not notice that. He was staring at the floor, slowly stroking his beard.

When the maid came back the judge went down on his knees and, with the kitchen knife, prised loose two slabs. The earth underneath was moist. He took the shovel and removed other slabs, piling them up by his side. He found six loose slabs, which together formed a rectangle of about five by three feet. Judge Dee rolled back his long sleeves, then began to shovel the loose earth away.

'You can't do such work, sir!' old Pan shouted aghast. 'Let me call a few servants!'

'Shut up!' snapped the judge. His shovel had struck something soft. As he went on, he noticed a nauseating smell coming up out of the hole. A piece of red leather became visible.

'There we have our missing clothes-box, Pan!' he exclaimed. He turned to the maid, who was squatting by the side of her mistress, trying to revive her. He shouted at her: 'Run to the gate! Tell the doorkeeper that Counsellor Pan orders him to go immediately to the tribunal and tell them that the counsellor wants the headman to come here right away with four constables and the matron of the jail. And, on your way back here, bring me a bundle of burning incense-sticks from the house altar! Get going!'

Judge Dee wiped the perspiration from his forehead. Pan had been looking unhappily at the prone figure of Mrs Ko. Now he asked diffidently:

'Shouldn't we make her more comfortable, sir? She——'

'No,' the judge said curtly. 'The cool floor is the best means of making her come to again. She knew very well that the corpse of her husband was buried under the floor here. She is the accomplice of a murderer.'

'But her husband jumped or fell into the river, sir. I myself saw him!'

132

'His body was never found, was it? I tell you that Ko Chih-yuan was murdered here in this room, when he came to take his medicine.'

'Who came rushing out of the house, then?'

'The murderer!' Judge Dee replied. Leaning with his arms on the shovel, he went on: 'It was a very clever scheme. When the murderer had buried Ko under the floor here, he put on Ko's robe and cap, and smeared his face with blood. Then he rushed out on the terrace and into the garden. All of you expected Ko to come out of the bedroom, and you saw the familiar robe and cap, and were alarmed by his shouting and the blood on his face. No wonder none of you realized it wasn't Ko. He first made for the pavilion, but he took good care not to come too near. Half-way he changed his direction, ran to the river-bank and jumped into the water. I suppose he let himself drift downstream till he saw a deserted spot on the bank, and climbed out. He threw the cap into the river, as a false clue.'

Pan nodded slowly.

'Yes,' he said, 'now I understand! But who could have been that man? Perhaps Kun-shan?'

'Kun-shan is indeed our most likely suspect,' Judge Dee replied. 'He must have stolen the banker's notebook after he had killed Ko. Kun-shan doesn't look very strong, but maybe he is a good swimmer.'

'He probably got that blood on his face by a self-inflicted wound,' Pan remarked.

'Or used Ko's blood. Here's the maid. Now we'll verify how Ko was killed. Take that burning incense from her, will you, and hold it close to my face!'

As Pan did so, the judge pulled up his neckcloth over his mouth and nose, and began shovelling the earth away from the lid of the red box. When the upper part of the box was free he knelt and ripped off the strip of oil-plaster that was pasted around the four sides of the lid. He righted himself and lifted the lid with the point of the shovel.

A foul smell came up. Pan quickly covered his nose with his sleeve and waved the incense so that they were enveloped in its blue cloud. The body of a frail man, clad only in an undergarment, was lying doubled up in the box. The grey head was bare, and the hilt of a knife protruded from under his left shoulder-blade. The judge turned the head a little with the point of the shovel, so that part of the wrinkled face became visible.

'Is it Ko Chih-yuan?' he asked.

When Pan nodded, his face contorted in speechless horror, the judge closed the box. He threw the shovel on the floor, then went over to the window and pushed it wide open. He set his cap right and wiped the sweat from his face.

'When your men get here,' he said to Pan, 'let them dig out the clothes-box and bring it to the tribunal as it is, with the corpse inside. Also order a closed palankeen. The matron will sit inside with Mrs Ko, and convey her to the tribunal to be locked up in a cell. Report everything to Magistrate Teng, and tell him that I am on my way to try to find and apprehend Kun-shan. If he isn't the murderer, he can at any rate give us valuable information. The magistrate had been planning to leave tomorrow morning for the Prefecture on urgent business, but after these new developments I think he'd better hear Mrs Ko first, during the morning session. If I succeed in catching Kun-shan, I trust we'll be able to close this case during that session, and then proceed to Pien-foo. I'll be off now. When you are back at the tribunal you'd better draw up a report concerning our discovery of the body. Tomorrow I'll sign it, as a witness.'

He took leave of Pan Yoo-te and told the maid to conduct him to the gate.

In the street it was still hot, but he thought that anything

134

was better than the foul atmosphere in the room he had just left. A strenuous uphill walk took him to the centre of the town. He felt hot and tired when he entered the alley of the Phoenix Inn.

Sounds of singing and laughter were coming through the window. The judge was pleased that everyone was still up and about, for now he could ask them for more information about Kun-shan. The waiter opened the door, looking more sour than ever. Apparently he had a dislike for late hours.

XIV

The taproom was lighted by half a dozen smoking candles; it presented a lively scene. Gambling was in full swing, the foursome had been reinforced by Chiao Tai and the Student, who lustily joined in the rhyming chorus when a particularly good combination was thrown. The Corporal sat in the rattan chair with Carnation on his knee, one arm round her waist and the other beating the time of the ribald song she was singing. When he saw the judge, he shouted:

'Hey thief-catcher, did you catch your man?'

'I didn't find the fellow, let alone catch him!' Judge Dee said sourly.

'The wench here says you caught her all right, though!' the Corporal said with a broad grin. 'From now on we shall call each other cousin, hey? All the same family!' He pushed the girl from his lap and got up. Slapping her behind he shouted: 'Now you'll show me what new tricks the beard taught you!'

They went laughing to the stairs.

Judge Dee sat down at the table near the window. Chiao Tai had risen and fetched two wine beakers from the counter. As he seated himself the judge asked eagerly:

'Did Kun-shan turn up?'

'Hasn't been near here!' Chiao Tai replied.

Judge Dee set his beaker down hard on the table. He said peevishly:

'I should have followed your advice! I made a bad mistake letting that fellow go! I can't understand why he hasn't turned up. He is clever enough, he must realize that, now that the tribunal has arrested Leng, they may issue a proclamation that all his possessions'll be confiscated, and that the gold shop then won't honour the drafts any more.' He called over to the gamblers: 'Hey there, do any of you know where I can find Kun-shan?'

The bald man looked round and shook his head.

'I don't think he has a fixed place to stay, brother, and if he has we never heard of it. He sleeps curled up under a stone, together with the other worms, I suppose!'

The gamblers guffawed.

'Has the scoundrel done more dirty things?' Chiao Tai asked.

'Perhaps a murder,' Judge Dee replied. Then he told Chiao Tai in a low voice what had happened at the Ko residence.

By the time he had finished, the four gamblers had settled accounts and were drifting towards the staircase. The Student went out. The waiter came up to Judge Dee's table and asked whether they would be needing him. When they said no, he disappeared behind the counter.

'Does that fellow sleep there?' Judge Dee asked, astonished.

'Certainly!' Chiao Tai said with a grin. 'He just fits into the second shelf. As regards Kun-shan now, much to my regret I must say that he couldn't have murdered old Ko, because he never could have managed that dive into the river. I've seen it. The current is very swift, jagged rocks stick out of the water everywhere, and there are plenty of nasty whirlpools. The man who dives into it, swims downstream and then comes out alive must not only know the river as well as the palm of his hand and have superior skill in swimming, but he must also have considerable strength and power of endurance. No, Magistrate, you can take my word for it—Kun-shan could never have done that.'

'In that case,' Judge Dee said, 'Kun-shan must have had an accomplice who jumped into the river. The scheme of the faked suicide itself bears the hallmark of Kun-shan's evil, tortuous mind. And, since he stole Leng Chien's notebook, he must have been there when the murder was committed. Tomorrow I'll tell Pan Yoo-te to send his best men out to arrest the scoundrel. He won't have left the city, not without the money or without trying to do us some dirty trick!'

'Talking about an accomplice,' Chiao Tai said slowly, 'when I visited Mrs Ko she told me that she had been expecting someone else, but that he hadn't turned up. Since I thought she was a courtesan, I took it that she referred to another customer. But it was probably her lover, and that man might be Kun-shan's helper! Heaven, that reminds me! She also said that she would be leaving town shortly!'

'She won't!' the judge remarked dryly. 'I had her put in jail, for she showed clearly that she knew about the murder. Tomorrow I'll ask Magistrate Teng to appoint me his temporary Assessor, so that I can take part in the questioning of Mrs Ko. Then, when the session is over, I shall accompany Teng on a trip to Pien-foo.' He told Chiao Tai about the two visits of the painter and his paramour to the house of assignation, about the mysterious person who had spied on them, and about his final conclusion that the woman had not been Mrs Teng at all. 'Therefore,' he said, 'I am glad that I made good progress with Ko Chih-yuan's case, I feel I owe that to the magistrate. Well, what did you find out this afternoon?'

'My job was easy. I left here after I had my little nap. That unpleasant youngster, the Student, insisted on accompanying me part of the way. He told me, very confidentially, about some big coup he is planning, all by himself, and which would net him two hundred gold pieces!'

'Not in two hundred years!' Judge Dee said. 'On our way to the marsh he dished out a similar tale to me. What did they say at headquarters about our kind host?'

'As usual,' Chiao Tai replied with a grin, 'I had to run around a bit before I found the right man. The officer in charge of personnel said that the files on deserters were with the military police, and the military police said that personnel had them. At last a clever sergeant took me apart and warned me that if I were going to wait for that file I'd have to wait till my hair had turned grey. But he knew that Captain Mao of the military police had served in the Third Wing of the Western Army too, and he thought that he might remember the case. Well, this Captain Mao is a nephew of Colonel Mao, of the fort in Peng-lai. He has the fiercest moustache I've ever seen in my life, but he proved to be a very likeable fellow notwithstanding, and he remembered our Corporal quite well. Mao said he had been an excellent soldier, several times commended for bravery in battle, and worshipped by his men. Thereafter, however, there came a new commanding officer, a certain Captain Woo, a crook who kept part of the soldiers' pay for himself. When a soldier protested, Woo ordered the Corporal to give him hundred lashes with the bowstring. The Corporal refused, and when Woo started beating him, the Corporal, he knocked Woo down. Since beating an officer is, of course, a capital offence, the Corporal took to his heels. Later it was discovered that Woo had accepted bribes from a secret agent of the barbarians, and he was beheaded. Captain Mao told me that if our Corporal had managed to stay out of mischief after his desertion, they would in this special case make an exception and forget about his offence. The army now needs good men like him, and if the magistrate recommends him, he'll be re-enlisted and promoted to sergeant. That's all.'

'I am glad to hear that,' Judge Dee said. 'The Corporal is a rough-and-ready rascal, but he has his heart in the right place. I'll see what I can do for him. Now, what about that soothsayer?'

'There can't be the slightest doubt that he is genuine. He's a dignified old man, very serious about his work. He had known Ko Chih-yuan for a long time, and liked him. He said old Ko was a bit nervous and fussy about small things, but a good and kind man, always ready to help others. I described Kun-shan to him, but he had never seen him. Then I asked the old gentleman to have a squint at my future too! He looked at my hand and said I would die by the sword. I told him that nothing would suit me better! But he didn't like that, for, as I said already, he's dead serious about his forecasts.'

'Well, that settles that!' the judge said. 'I reckoned with the possibility that someone who wished to harm Ko had bribed the soothsayer to indicate the fifteenth as a dangerous day, so as to be able to lay his plans beforehand. Now we'd better be off to bed, for we'll have to be at the tribunal early. This is our last night here in the Phoenix Inn, Chiao Tai. Tomorrow I'll have to give up my incognito. We'll stay in the guest quarters of the tribunal for the rest of my leave.'

Chiao Tai took the candle, and they went upstairs.

They found their small bedroom even hotter and closer than the night before. Judge Dee would have opened the window, but the myriad tiny thuds resounding from outside against the dirty oil-paper reminded him that clouds of winged insects were waiting for the assault. With a sigh he lay down on the hard couch, pulling his robe close so as to be protected somewhat against the other hordes that presently would come crawling from the crevices among the planks. Chiao Tai again stretched himself out on the floor, his head close to the door.

Judge Dee turned and tossed on the plank-bed, but sleep would not come. Soon he found that the air had become suffocating. Since, now that he had doused the candle, there

140

seemed to be fewer flying insects attacking the window, he decided to open it. But he pulled and pushed in vain; it had become stuck in its frame. He took the hair-needle out of his top-knot, and, with its sharp point, cut the oil-paper from the square window panes. A slight breeze came in, together with the cool rays of the moon, and he felt somewhat relieved. He again lay down on the plank-bed, and put his neck-cloth over his face to protect himself against the mosquitoes. After a while his fatigue asserted itself, and he fell asleep.

Except for the rhythmic snoring, the Phoenix Inn was still.

XV

Chiao Tai woke up with a start. There was a strange, pungent smell in his nose. The year of city life as Judge Dee's assistant had not yet dulled the alertness of his senses, acquired during the years he had lived in the 'green woods'. He sneezed, and immediately thought of a fire, and of the fact that the inn consisted of boards. He jumped up, grabbed Judge Dee's foot and threw himself against the door, all in one and the same moment. The door burst open and he tumbled into the narrow passage outside, dragging the judge with him. He collided in the dark with a queer, slippery shape. He grabbed at it but missed. There was the sound of someone falling down the staircase. Something clattered on the wooden stairs, then there came suppressed groans from down below. Chiao Tai began to cough. He shouted:

'Get up! There's a fire!' And, to the judge: 'Downstairs, quick!'

Bedlam followed. While cursing, half-naked men came crowding into the passage, Chiao Tai and the judge let themselves slide down the stairs. Below, Chiao Tai stumbled over a human body, scrambled up again, ran to the door and kicked it wide open. He took a deep breath, then he went coughing and sneezing to the counter, groped for a tinder-box and lit a candle. Judge Dee rushed outside into the street too. He was dizzy and nauseated, but after he had sneezed a couple of times he felt better. He looked up at the second storey, but all was dark there. The place was not on fire, but he thought he knew what had happened. When he went inside again the waiter had emerged with tousled head from behind the counter and was lighting more candles.

Their light shone on a weird scene. The Corporal, stark naked and looking like a huge, hairy ape, stood with the bald man over a queer, whimpering figure, sitting on the floor and nursing its left leg. Its naked body was glistening with oil. The three gamblers, scantily dressed, were looking dazedly at each other with watering eyes. Carnation, clutching a small loin cloth round her naked body, stared with horrified eyes at the groaning man on the floor. Judge Dee, who, with Chiao Tai, was the only person fully dressed, stooped and picked up a bamboo blowpipe about two feet long, which had a small gourd attached to its end. He hurriedly examined it, then he barked at Kunshan:

'What poison did you blow into our room?'

'It was no poison, only a sleeping drug!' Kun-shan whined. 'It was nothing, I didn't want to hurt any of you! I have broken my ankle!'

The Corporal gave him a vicious kick in the ribs.

'I'll break every bone in your body!' he growled. 'What do you mean by sneaking in here, you son of a dog?'

'He wanted to rob me,' Judge Dee said. He looked at Chiao Tai, who was searching a pile of clothes that lay next to the door. 'You can close the door,' he called out to him, 'the particles of powder this rascal blew into the room have dispersed by now.' And, to the Corporal: 'Look, the bastard undressed down here and oiled his body so that he could wriggle out of the hands of anyone trying to catch him. He planned to flee after he had stolen what he could!'

'That makes it simple,' the Corporal said. 'I am against killings but, as the rule says that a man who steals from his comrades shall die, we'll finish him off. But you go ahead and question him. You have the first claim!'

He gave a sign to his men. They grabbed Kun-shan, and pinned him spread-eagled to the floor, standing on his hands and feet. Kun-shan screamed when the bald man planted a foot on his broken ankle, but the Corporal started to kick him again.

Judge Dee raised his hand. He stared curiously at the prone man. His horribly emaciated body was covered with long, evil looking scars that seemed to have been caused by burns. Chiao Tai came up to the judge and handed him two packages he had found in Kun-shan's clothes. Judge Dee gave the heavy one back to Chiao Tai, and opened the other. It contained a water-stained notebook. 'Where did you steal this?' he asked the man on the floor.

'I found it!' Kun-shan screamed.

'Tell the truth!' Judge Dee barked.

'It is the truth!'

'Get a shovel of burning coal and a pair of fire-tongs from the kitchen!' the Corporal snapped at the waiter. 'We'll just lay a few of those hot coals on this bastard's belly. That's always a good start. It'll smell a bit, but you can't have everything.'

'No! Don't burn me!' Kun-shan shouted frantically. 'I found it, I swear it!'

'Where?' the judge asked.

'Here! The other night, I came here and searched all the rooms upstairs while you were sleeping. I found it behind that woman's bed!'

Judge Dee quickly looked at Carnation. Clutching her naked breast, she suppressed a cry. Seeing the frantic entreaty in her eyes, in a flash he understood. He said hurriedly to the Corporal:

'It's no use, the bastard is lying. I and my mate'd better take him to a quiet spot and have a leisurely talk with him. If we do it here he may become a bit noisy, and there's no

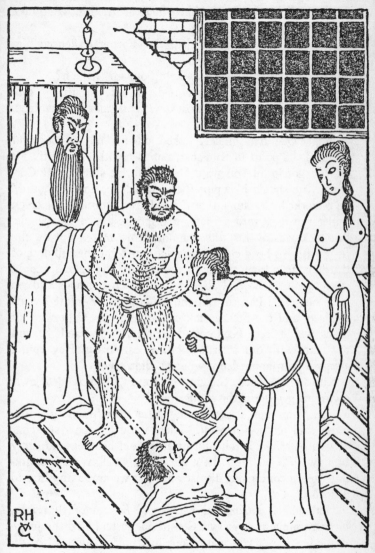

COMMOTION IN THE PHOENIX INN

need to tell the whole neighbourhood about this. We'll take him out to the marsh.'

'No, no!' Kun-shan wailed. The Corporal silenced him with a kick. He snarled:

'The dirty dogshead! Slandering our girl too, eh?'

'It's true!' Kun-shan shouted. 'I tell you that I tore out a few pages, then put it back. When I came here tonight, I——'

Judge Dee had quickly taken off his felt slipper and rammed the point in Kun-shan's open mouth. 'Presently I'll let you gossip all you want!' he said. He showed the Corporal Kun-shan's blowpipe. 'The powder is in this gourd,' he remarked. 'I assume that if you blow it through the crack under the door into a room, it disperses and drugs people. But luck was against the scoundrel. My mate slept on the floor with his head close to the door, and got the full dose of the powder in his face. He sneezed it out, and before it could start to spread he had already burst open the door and we were outside. I had cut out the window paper before I went to sleep, and the breeze took care of the rest. Otherwise all of us would have been sound asleep by now, and me and my mate with our throats slit from ear to ear. Hey you, I suppose you jammed my window, didn't you?'

Kun-shan nodded. Gagging he moved his distended jaws, trying to get rid of the slipper.

'Let your men paste an oil-plaster over his mouth,' the judge said to the Corporal. 'Then, if they make a stretcher of two poles, we'll roll him up in an old blanket, and carry him away. If we meet the nightwatch, we'll say he is suffering from a contagious disease and that we are taking him to a doctor.'

'Baldy!' the Corporal bellowed. 'Let go of that foot, he can't move it anyway! Get an oil-plaster!' To the judge he said: 'Don't you want some instruments along?'

146

'I have been a headman, so I know my job!' Judge Dee replied. 'You might lend me a knife, though.'

'Good!' the Corporal said. 'That reminds me! I would like his ears and fingers, please. I'll send them around to a few people in this city who are getting a bit fresh, just as a little warning. Bring them back in a piece of oil-paper, will you? And where are you going to hide the body?'

'We'll bury it in the quicksand of the marsh. It'll never be found.'

'Excellent!' the Corporal said, gratified. 'I don't like killings here as a rule, but if there has to be one, I like it to be a workmanlike job!'

Kun-shan's eyes, crazy with pain and fear, were bulging from his head. He was wriggling like an eel under the men's feet. When the bald gambler pulled the slipper out of his mouth he began making incoherent sounds, but immediately the sticky plaster was clapped over his mouth. The Corporal himself bound his hands and legs together with a thin rope. Carnation brought an old blanket, and she helped Chiao Tai to roll the thin man up in it from head to feet. Two men had brought an improvised stretcher, and Kun-shan was secured to it with more ropes.

Judge Dee and Chiao Tai lifted the stretcher and put the poles on their shoulders.

The Student came in. He looked, astonished, at the men and the naked girl, then asked:

'What's going on here?'

'None of your business, runt!' the Corporal growled. And, to Judge Dee:

'There's nobody about near that marsh at night, so take your time over him. I never trusted that ugly bastard!'

The judge and Chiao Tai went out into the alley, carrying their burden. If the neighbours had noticed all the commotion, they thought it wiser not to give any sign of it.

Two streets farther on they met the nightwatch. Judge Dee said curtly to their headman:

'Help us to get this man to the tribunal. He's a dangerous criminal.'

Two sturdy watchmen took the stretcher from them.

At the main entrance of the tribunal, Judge Dee gave his card to the sleepy guard and told him to rouse Counsellor Pan. The watchmen put the stretcher down in the gatehouse and left. Soon the guard came back, carrying a lighted lampion. Pan followed him, clad in a house-robe. He started to ask questions agitatedly, but Judge Dee cut him short.

'I have Kun-shan here,' he said. 'Tell the guards to take him to your private office. And call Magistrate Teng. I'll explain later!'

When the guards had deposited the stretcher on the floor in Pan's office, Judge Dee told them to bring a jar of warm wine. He and Chiao Tai freed Kun-shan from the blanket, cut his ropes with the Corporal's knife, and placed him in an armchair. The judge turned it round so that it faced the wall. Kun-shan wanted to raise his hands to take the plaster from his mouth, but the cruel thin ropes had bitten deeply into the flesh, and he could not move them. He began to groan. The light of the single candle shone on his distorted face, and his thin, scarred body. His left ankle was swollen, the foot bent at an unnatural angle.

Chiao Tai remarked:

'That broken ankle of his gives me an idea. Suppose that this is the dirty peeper who followed the couple to the house of assignation, and that he faked a limp? That would be a good disguise. And the rest fits, he is tall and thin enough!'

Judge Dee swung round and stared fixedly at his lieutenant.

'Well,' Chiao Tai said diffidently, 'it's only an idea, but I——'

'Shut up!' Judge Dee barked at him. He began pacing the floor, angrily muttering to himself. Chiao Tai looked at him unhappily, wondering what he had done wrong.

The judge stood still. He said gravely:

'Thank you, Chiao Tai! Your remark has made me discover the truth. I have been a fool, stared myself blind on one interpretation. . . . Well, now my problem is solved.'

He heard footsteps in the corridor, and quickly went outside, motioning Chiao Tai to stay with the prisoner.

Magistrate Teng was clad in a house-robe, just as Pan Yoo-te. His eyes were heavy with sleep. He wanted to ask something, but Judge Dee said in a low voice:

'Send your counsellor away!'

When Teng had given Pan a short order, the judge went on:

'Tomorrow you'll hear the prisoner in the tribunal, Teng. The rules forbid a magistrate to question a man in private. But that rule doesn't apply to me here, and I'll hear him now. You'll stand behind his chair so that he can't see you.'

A guard appeared, carrying a tray with a jar of wine and two cups. Judge Dee took it from him, and stepped back into the room. He pulled a chair up to Kun-shan's side and sat down, holding the wine-jar and a cup in his hands. Magistrate Teng and Chiao Tai remained standing by the desk. Judge Dee looked round at Chiao Tai and gave him a sign to lock the door. Then he ripped the plaster from Kun-shan's mouth.

Kun-shan moved his misshapen mouth convulsively. He stammered: 'Don't . . . don't . . .'

'You won't be tortured, Kun-shan. I promise you,' the judge said in a soft, persuasive voice. 'I am a special agent, Kun-shan, I saved you from those cruel men there at the inn. Here, drink some wine!' He brought the beaker to Kun-shan's mouth, and let him drink. Then he pulled loose his own neck-cloth and laid it over the naked man's lap. 'Later I'll give you a clean robe, and I'll have a physician look at your ankle, Kun-shan. Then you'll have a nice, long sleep. You must be very tired, and your ankle hurts badly, doesn't it?'

The sudden change from the brutal scene in the inn unnerved Kun-shan completely. He began to cry softly, tears came rolling down his hollow cheeks. Judge Dee took an oblong package from his bosom. He unwrapped it and showed Kun-shan the antique dagger. He asked in the same soothing voice:

'Was this dagger hanging over the dressing-table, Kun-shan?'

'No, it hung by the bed, next to the lute,' Kun-shan replied. Judge Dee let him drink from the beaker again.

'My ankle!' Kun-shan groaned. 'It's hurting so much!'

'Don't worry, Kun-shan, we'll look after that. You'll feel better soon. You won't be tortured, I promise you. They burned you badly before, didn't they?'

'They burned me with hot irons!' Kun-shan cried. 'And I was innocent, it was that woman who called them!'

'That was a long time ago, Kun-shan. You've killed a woman now, and you'll have to die, of course, but I'll make everything easy for you. I promise that they won't torture you. Nobody'll touch you.'

'She seduced me, the lewd slut, she seduced me, I tell you! Just like that harlot before, she seduced me! And see what they did, how they burned me, look at my body!'

'Why did they burn you, Kun-shan?'

'I was still so young, just a boy. . . . I passed that house, and the girl smiled at me, from behind the window. She invited me, I tell you! But when I went inside, she said she had only laughed at my ugly face . . . I wanted her, she screamed, I grabbed her by the throat, I . . . I . . . She hit me in the face with a wine-jar. It broke and cut my cheek, the jagged end pierced my eye. Look at the scar, you can see it for yourself! Then the men came. She shouted I had tried to rape her. They threw me on the floor, they burned me. . . . When they ran off to get the constables, I managed to escape. . . .'

He burst into convulsive sobs. Judge Dee silently let him drink again. Kun-shan began to tremble all over. He said with chattering teeth:

'I have never touched a woman again, never, in all those years. Till . . . till that other slut seduced me. I didn't want it, I only wanted the money, I swear it! You must believe me, please!'

'Had you been to the magistrate's house before, Kun-shan?' the judge asked calmly.

'Only once, also during the siesta. That's the best time, for at night there are the guards. I went in by the emergency entrance. She was in the library, the bedroom was empty. I searched the room, found the safe behind the dressing-table, then I heard someone coming. I left by the garden door, climbed onto the roof, and let myself down into the empty back street.'

'How did you enter the second time?'

'By way of the roof and the small garden. I blew the powder under the garden door, and waited. When I entered, the maid was lying on the bamboo couch, drugged. I went to the bedroom to open the safe. Then I saw her lying on the bed there, also drugged. She was lying there all naked, the slut! I tell you I didn't want to do it, but . . . I had to. Why didn't she cover herself up decently, why should she lie there naked like a whore? She seduced me, she soiled me! And then she taunted me, with that still face, her eyes closed! I took the dagger and stuck it in her evil breast. I

151

wanted to cut her to pieces, destroy that evil, lewd woman. . . .'

He suddenly halted. Sweat was streaming down his haggard face, and running quickly along his oiled breast. His one eye fixing the judge with a crazed expression, he went on softly:

'I heard a door close somewhere in the house. I quickly went to the dressing-room. The maid was still drugged, but I heard footsteps approaching in the corridor. I emptied all the powder from my blowpipe there, then fled through the garden door, pulling it closed behind me. I crawled over the roofs, stumbled on through the street until I saw the teahouse. It was early, only the waiter was on the terrace. I told him I was ill, and fell into a chair. When I had drunk several cups of tea, I recovered somewhat. Then I knew I had to leave this accursed place, where I had been soiled, humiliated. . . . I had to get Leng Chien's money as quickly as possible. Then I would flee . . . go to a far-away place, to get clean again. I saw you two coming, you left, and I studied your companion. When you came back and had tea there, I again observed you, both of you. I knew you two could get the money from Leng. I followed you to the hostel, I . . .'

'Yes, I know,' Judge Dee interrupted him. 'I also know how you got the notebook. You found it in the girl's room, and first tore out only a few pages. Tonight you stole it. All that doesn't matter now. Now we must only think how we can make it easy for you. Shall I tell you how we'll do it? We'll arrange your killing Mrs Teng as a simple murder. If you confess that you raped her too, Kun-shan, they'll torture you. They'll condemn you to the lingering death. You know how the executioner begins, don't you? He starts with cutting slices from your breast, and . . .'

'No!' Kun-shan screamed. 'Help me!'

'Yes, I'll help you. But you must listen very carefully, and do exactly as I say, Kun-shan. You must say that you knew that Mrs Teng often went to visit her elder sister, in her villa outside the north gate. You entered by the small garden, and when you saw that the maid was away, you knocked. You told Mrs Teng that her sister needed her immediately, for an urgent and secret family affair. You said her sister was in great trouble, and that she had to bring ten gold pieces, and not to tell anybody, not even her husband. She believed you, took the money and went with you, leaving by the secret door. The street was deserted during the siesta, so you could take her unnoticed through the ruins to the marsh. There you told her to hand the gold and the jewels to you. She wanted to call for help. You became afraid; pulling your dagger, you told her to shut up. She tried to wrest the dagger from you, and before you knew it you had stabbed her to death. You tore her earrings off and took her bracelets and the package with the gold. The gold you spent, but you didn't dare to dispose of the jewels. Here they are. They'll be brought forward as evidence.'

He took them from his sleeve, and showed them to Kun-shan. Then he resumed:

'Keep to that story, Kun-shan. I guarantee that then they won't beat you, they won't question you under torture. You'll die, but it'll be a quick death. Then all your troubles will be over, Kun-shan, and you needn't fear anything any more. They'll give you a good bed, now, and a doctor will look at your ankle. Then you'll have a few hours of nice sleep. They'll hear you during the morning session. You tell your story, and then no one will bother you any more for many days. For many days and nights you can rest, Kun-shan, rest . . .'

The thin man made no response. His head was sinking slowly to his breast. He was completely exhausted.

Judge Dee rose. He whispered to Chiao Tai:

'Call the guards and let the warden of the jail lock him up. See to it that a physician treats his ankle, and gives him a drug.' He motioned Teng to follow him outside.

The magistrate's face was of a deadly pallor. He started to mutter something about his gratitude, but the judge quickly interrupted him, saying:

'I hope you'll allow me to stay here at the tribunal to-night.'

'Certainly, Dee! Anything you wish!' Teng took him to the courtyard outside. 'It was . . . unspeakable, Dee!'

'Quite,' Judge Dee said dryly. 'Would you summon your counsellor now, and tell him to assign twelve constables to my lieutenant? They'll have to go now and arrest the boss of the underworld here, called The Corporal, and a young hoodlum called The Student.'

'Of course!'

The magistrate clapped his hands, and, when the frightened-looking Pan appeared, told him to have the guest quarters prepared for the judge, and to follow his orders regarding two arrests. He added with a bleak smile:

'If you stay here long enough, Dee, my jail will be too small!'

'We'll hear the prisoners tomorrow morning,' Judge Dee said with an impassive face. 'I beg you to appoint me your Assessor at the start of the session, so that I can question some of them personally. Good night!'

He gave Pan and Chiao Tai his instructions. Then a servant led him to the guest quarters, behind the large reception hall.

He saw that the guest-room was large and comfortable. He sat down in an armchair, aimlessly following the movements of two servants as they lighted the large silver candelabra on the high wall table, and drew open the silken curtains of the bedstead of carved rosewood. The old steward came in with a large tray of tea and cold refreshments, followed by a sleepy maid who hung a clean bed-robe on the rack of red lacquer. The steward poured him a cup of hot tea, then lit a stick of incense in front of the large landscape painting that decorated the side wall. He bowed, wished the judge an obsequious good night, and left.

Judge Dee leaned back in the armchair and slowly sipped his tea. Then, with a tired gesture, he lifted his left arm and took from his sleeve Kun-shan's blowpipe. With a sigh he put it on the table. He ought to have thought of that possibility. The chambermaid who slept through all the commotion, not waking up even when Teng let the vase shatter on the marble floor, the serene face of the dead woman—those facts should have told him at once that they had been drugged. And there had been no coincidence. Magistrate Teng had not had an attack of insanity, he had been overpowered by the large dose of the drug that Kun-shan had released in the dressing-room just before he fled. And Mrs Teng had been dead already when her husband entered the dressing-room and saw her through the bedroom door that stood ajar.

He vaguely heard the wooden gong of the nightwatch passing through the street outside the tribunal. In a few hours it would be dawn. He didn't think he could sleep.

His eye fell on the elegant small book-rack of polished bamboo standing in the corner. He got up and selected a volume bound in costly brocade. He opened it and found it was a special edition of Magistrate Teng's poetry, printed on the most expensive paper, glossy as white jade. With an angry exclamation he pushed it back among the other books. He took another volume at random, and sat down with it. It was a Buddhist text. Slowly he read the beginning aloud:

'To be born means suffering and sorrow,
  To live means suffering and sorrow,
  To die, and never be reborn, is the only deliverance
  Of all suffering and sorrow.'

He closed the book. As a follower of Confucius he was not
partial to Buddhist teachings. But the lines he had just read
accorded surprisingly well with his present mood.

He fell asleep as he was sitting there, with the book in
his lap.

XVI

Chiao Tai came to report shortly after dawn, when Judge Dee was making his toilet. He said, while the judge was combing his beard:

'The Corporal and the Student are under lock and key, in the jail here. At one moment it looked as if there was going to be a bad fight. The bald man and the others drew their knives and wanted to defend the Corporal. But he barked at them: "Didn't I tell you I want no knife fighting? I am through, Baldy takes over!" Then he let the constables put the chains on him.'

Judge Dee nodded. He said:

'I have one more task for you. Borrow a horse from the guards and go to the country house of Mrs Teng's elder sister, outside the north gate. Find out where Mrs Teng's two other sisters are living. Then, on your way back, buy two bolts of superior silk, as used for ladies' dresses, in a good silk shop. Here is some money.' He gave Chiao Tai ten silver pieces, and added: 'If you are back before the session of the tribunal is over, you can join me behind the bench and follow the proceedings!'

Chiao Tai hastily took his leave, for he was eager to attend the session. Judge Dee drank a cup of hot tea, then walked over to Pan Yoo-te's office.

The old counsellor told him that Magistrate Teng had left it to Judge Dee to prepare the morning session. The judge asked:

'Did you draw up the report of our discovering Ko's body?'

Pan gave him a few sheets of paper. The judge read them

through carefully. He corrected a few sentences in such a manner that all the credit for the discovery went to Pan, then signed and sealed the documents. Handing the papers back, he said:

'After I have been installed as Assessor, Magistrate Teng will hear Kun-shan. I shall interfere only if the accused should try to prevaricate. Then I myself shall hear Mrs Ko, and finally the magistrate and I together shall hear the banker Leng Chien. Here you have two drafts, each for three hundred and fifty gold pieces. They represent about two-thirds of the money Leng Chien stole from Ko Chih-yuan. Fill in the Ko estate as payee; the money rightfully belongs to them.' He took from his sleeve the heavy package that Chiao Tai had found in Kun-shan's sleeve. Opening it, he continued: 'Here are four gold bars, to the value of two hundred gold pieces. It was Ko's emergency fund, but Kun-shan stole it from Ko's safe. Transfer this gold to the Ko estate too. There remain three hundred gold pieces which Leng deposited with the Heavenly Rain gold shop. Have it confiscated, to be restored to the Ko family also, in due time.'

Pan wrote out receipts for the drafts and the gold. Handing the documents to the judge, he said with a grateful smile:

'You found the culprit and recovered all the money, sir! How is it possible that you achieved all that in such a short time?'

'There were helpful circumstances,' Judge Dee said vaguely. 'Could you lend me a decent robe and cap to wear in court?'

The counsellor called a clerk. He came back with a long robe of blue damask and a black velvet cap with gold braid. Judge Dee put the robe on over his own, stuffed his worn cap in his sleeve and placed the gold-rimmed one on his head. In this dignified attire he walked back to the guest quarters and ordered a simple breakfast from the steward.

When he had laid down his chopsticks he went out into the small rock garden behind his bedroom and walked round it, his hands behind his back. He felt tired and restless. At last three loud beats on the bronze gong at the main gate announced that the morning session of the tribunal was about to begin.

He found Magistrate Teng waiting for him in his private office behind the court hall. Teng wore his green official robe, and the winged black judge's cap. Together they passed through the unicorn screen-curtain and ascended the dais. Teng insisted that Judge Dee sit on his right.

The news of the night's commotion in Ko Chih-yuan's residence, and the arrest of Mrs Ko and the others, had spread through the entire city. The court hall was packed with a dense crowd. Many more spectators who had not been able to obtain a place inside jostled each other just outside the entrance of the hall.

When Magistrate Teng had called the roll, he started filling out the forms which made Judge Dee Assessor of the court. Pausing with lifted writing-brush, he asked:

'How many days shall I put in for the term of your assignment, Dee?'

'One,' the judge replied. 'Today only.'

Teng signed and sealed the forms, and passed them on to Judge Dee, who did the same. Then Magistrate Teng wrote out a slip for the warden of the jail, and Kun-shan was led before the bench. Two constables had to support him by his arms. His ankle had been put in a splint. The thin man looked more dead than alive. Judge Dee remembered Chiao Tai's description when they had seen Kun-shan for the first time, on the terrace of the teahouse: a loathsome insect that has just crawled out of its shell.

After the formal questions about his name and profession, Teng stated that the court accused Kun-shan of murder and robbery. Kun-shan recited his confession, exactly as Judge Dee had instructed him. Once he lost the thread of his narrative, but the magistrate brought him onto the right track again with a few skilful questions.

Kun-shan heard his confession read out by the senior scribe, agreed that it was correct and affixed his thumb-mark to it. Magistrate Teng pronounced him guilty of the two crimes cited, and condemned him to death by decapitation. Kun-shan was led back to the jail. There he would wait for the final sentence, which in due time would be forthcoming from the metropolitan court in the capital, which had to ratify all capital punishments. A confused noise rose from the audience. Some shouted invectives at the criminal, others protested their sympathy and admiration for Magistrate Teng.

Teng rapped his gavel. Judge Dee whispered to him:

'I would like to have Mrs Ko called now.'

Teng filled out a slip, and presently the matron of the jail led Mrs Ko before the bench. She had pulled her hair straight back and done it up in a simple chignon, with a green jade comb as her only ornament. She had not powdered or rouged her face, and in the straight white robe she looked like a sedate housewife. As she slowly knelt down on the stone floor, Judge Dee asked himself worriedly whether he had made a mistake after all.

After Teng had put the routine questions to her, he stated that the Assessor would now conduct the questioning. Judge Dee spoke:

'Last night, Mrs Ko, the dead body of your husband was discovered under the floor of his bedroom, in your presence. Pan Yoo-te, counsellor of this tribunal, and I myself are prepared to testify that you gave proof of knowing that the body had been buried there. Before this court formulates its case against you, you shall give a circumstantial account of

160

what happened on the night of the fifteenth, after your husband had left the dinner in the pavilion and entered the house.'

Mrs Ko raised her head and began in a soft but clear voice:

'This person pleads guilty. She is guilty because she did not at once report to this tribunal the terrible truth. I can only hope that the court will deign to remember that I am only a weak and ignorant woman who has always led a secluded life, and therefore view my case with leniency.'

She paused a moment. A murmur of sympathy rose from the audience. Magistrate Teng rapped his gavel and called for order. Mrs Ko went on:

'How many times have I lived through again, in my feverish nightmares, those agonizing moments! I had gone from my boudoir to my husband's bedroom, to see whether the servants hadn't forgotten to lay out his bed-robe. When I was standing near the table, I suddenly felt that I was not alone. When I turned round, the bed-curtains opened and a man sprang into the room. I wanted to shout for help, but he raised a long, evil-looking knife, and I could only moan, frozen with fright. He stepped up to me and——'

'Describe that man, madam!' Judge Dee interrupted her.

'He had wound a thin blue veil all around his head, Your Honour. He was tall and thin and he was wearing—I can hardly remember, I was so frightened—yes, I believe he wore a blue jacket and trousers, as workmen do . . .'

The judge nodded and she continued:

'Standing very close to me, he hissed: "One sound and . . ." He pressed the point of the knife against my breast. "Soon your husband will come in," he went on in that horrible, muffled voice. "Talk to him, do whatever he says." Just then I heard footsteps in the passageway that leads to the terrace. The man quickly jumped towards the door and pressed his back against the wall next to it. My husband

161

entered, saw me, opened his mouth to speak . . . Then the man suddenly struck him down from behind . . .'

She buried her face in her hands and began to sob. On Judge Dee's sign the headman gave her a bowl of strong tea. She greedily drank it. Then she went on:

'I must have fainted. When I came to, my husband wasn't there, I saw only his robe and cap lying on a chair. The man put them on. That face, that terrible masked face, above the familiar robe of my husband . . . And the blood, the veil was soaked with blood . . . The man whispered: "Your husband is dead, he killed himself, you understand? If you ever open your mouth, I'll cut your throat!" He pushed me roughly towards the door. I stumbled through the empty corridor to my boudoir. I had barely sunk down on my couch when I heard loud cries in the garden outside. The servants were shouting that my husband had drowned himself, thrown himself into the river. I wanted to tell the truth, Your Honour, I swear I wanted to! But, just as I had made up my mind to go to this tribunal, I saw again that fearful mask, covered with blood . . . and I dared not. I know I am guilty, Your Honour, but I didn't dare . . .'

Again she burst out sobbing.

'You may rise and stand back, madam!' Judge Dee spoke. The matron helped Mrs Ko up. She remained standing against the desk of the clerk, to the left of the bench, staring vacantly ahead. Judge Dee bent over to Magistrate Teng and said:

'Have Hsia Liang called now, please.'

Two constables brought a young man before the bench. He was clad in a jacket, open at the neck, and blue baggy trousers. Judge Dee thought he looked as sullen as when he had seen him first, in the taproom of the Phoenix Inn. When the Student saw the judge he stiffened. Then his eye fell on Mrs Ko, who gave him a cold stare. Slowly he knelt down.

'State your name and profession!' the judge ordered.

'This person is called Hsia, named Liang,' the young man replied in a steady voice. 'Graduate of the town school.'

'Dare you announce your literary grade?' Judge Dee barked at him. 'You who have brought shame on the literary class and committed the sordid crime you stand accused of? That woman has just made a full confession!'

'This person,' the Student said calmly, 'doesn't know what crime Your Honour refers to. And he never saw that woman before.'

Judge Dee was vexed. He had counted on the Student breaking down when he saw him sitting behind the bench, and was confronted unexpectedly with Mrs Ko. Apparently he had underrated the youngster's presence of mind. He said curtly:

'Rise, Hsia Liang, and face that woman!' Then he asked Mrs Ko: 'Do you recognize this man as the murderer of your husband?'

Mrs Ko looked steadily at the Student. For one brief moment their eyes met. Then she said, slowly and very clearly:

'How could I? I told Your Honour that the intruder wore a mask!'

'In deference to your late husband,' Judge Dee spoke, 'this court wished to give you full opportunity for clearing yourself. Although it is up to the accused to prove his innocence, this court even brought forward a suspect for you to identify. Since the explanation you gave is evidently a false story, the court now formulates its case. You stand accused of having murdered your husband, Mrs Ko, together with an accomplice as yet unknown. Headman, you can release the witness Hsia Liang!'

'Wait! Let me think, please!' Mrs Ko cried out. She again looked at the Student, biting her lips. After some hesitation she went on: 'Yes, the build seems similar. . . . But I can't tell about the face, of course. . . ."

'That is not enough, madam!' the judge said quickly. 'You must supply concrete proof!'

'Yes,' Mrs Ko said in a faltering voice, 'since there was all that blood, on the veil . . .' Suddenly she looked up at the judge and said: 'If he is the murderer, he must have a wound on his head!'

Judge Dee gave a sign to the headman. He grabbed the young man by his shoulders and roughly pulled his head back. The forelock fell away, and a badly healed cut became visible at the root of his hair.

'It is he,' Mrs Ko said, very softly. She buried her face in her hands.

The Student tried to wrench himself loose. His face scarlet with rage, he shouted:

'You treacherous slut!'

'The man is crazy!' Mrs Ko cried out. 'Make that mean beggar stop his foul language, Your Honour!'

'Beggar?' the Student screamed. 'It was you who begged me, begged me to love you! But, fool that I was, I didn't see what you were after! You only wanted to use me to kill your husband, eh, so that you could get hold of his money and then get rid of me! And it was you who took those two hundred gold pieces, of course!'

Mrs Ko began to protest, but he shouted at her:

'Of course you did! And I, who can get any young girl I want, I forced myself to make love to you, you who are years older than me! Heaven, I hated it, but, fool that I was, I——'

'Don't say that, Liang!' Mrs Ko cried out. She gripped the edge of the table behind her to steady herself, and repeated forlornly: 'Liang, you should not have said that! I loved you . . .' Her voice trailed off. She spoke very softly when she resumed: 'Yes, perhaps I knew it, though . . . knew it all the time. But I didn't want to know it, I thought that, perhaps, you really . . .' Suddenly she burst into shrill laughter and cried: 'Just now I even thought that you would sacrifice yourself for me!' The laughter changed into sobbing. Then she wiped her face. Raising her head she looked steadily at the judge and said in a clear voice: 'That man was my lover. He killed my husband, and I was his accomplice!' Turning again to the Student, who was staring at her, dumbfounded, she said softly: 'Now we'll go together, Liang . . . together . . . at last.'

She leaned back against the table with closed eyes, panting heavily.

'Hsia Liang, make your confession!' Judge Dee spoke.

The Student slowly shook his head, half-dazed. He muttered:

'That woman . . . she's ruined me, the crazy fool!'

The headman pressed him down roughly on his knees. The Student resumed in a hoarse voice:

'Yes, I murdered the merchant Ko, but I tell you that she made me do it! I only wanted to rob the place. The men in the inn were always taunting me, saying that I couldn't do the simplest job. I knew there was a tree outside the wall of Ko's house, I decided it would be easy to break in. I would show the men what I could do! Show them real gold! About two months ago I heard from the servants that Ko would be away for a few days. To climb over the wall was child's play. I enter a room, and feel about in the dark. I suddenly bump into a woman. Heaven, was I frightened! My first job, and then such dirty luck! They had told me no one lived in that wing when the master was away. What if she starts to shout? I grab her and clasp my hand over her mouth. The moon comes out, and we look at each other. I growl nervously: "Where's the money?" I feel her lips moving under my hand. I take it away. She is not afraid, not she! She laughs! Well, I stay there that night—she lets me go only when dawn is breaking. She gives me some money.'

As he paused and rubbed his hand over his face, Judge Dee said:

'If you remain silent, Mrs Ko, the court assumes that you agree with this man's statement. Have you any remarks?'

Mrs Ko, who had been looking fixedly at the Student, now shook her head listlessly.

'Proceed!' Judge Dee ordered the Student.

'Well, after that I went to visit her regularly. She told me a lot about how rich her husband was, but that he was very stingy, and never let her have enough money. She said he kept all the keys, and therefore she couldn't give me more. I said I didn't care about such chicken-feed. Then she said her husband always kept two hundred gold pieces in his safe. If he were out of the way, we could take those and flee to some distant place together. Well, two hundred in gold is good money, but murder isn't a small matter. If we do it at all, I said, we must do it well, there's no hurry. But she kept urging me, she said she hated the life she was leading. Then I worked out a good plan. I gave her a box with arsenic and taught her how she could give her husband a small dose in his morning tea every other day, just enough to cause a stomach ache. I also gave her a powder to make the pain subside. Wasn't the old fool grateful to her, that she looked after him so well! All his own fault! He shouldn't have married a lewd woman!'

Mrs Ko uttered a suppressed cry, but he ignored her and continued:

'The other day she tells me that a soothsayer has warned Ko that on the fifteenth he'll be in danger of his life. She says that that's nonsense of course, but we can use it for executing our plan. It'll do nicely as a motive for suicide. She coaxes him into giving a dinner that night. Before he goes to the pavilion, she gives him a good dose of the arsenic. I climb over the wall. She has sent all the servants to the other wing, to help with the dinner preparations. We push the bedstead away, I dig the hole. When we replace the bed, the earth and the loose slabs are safely underneath. Then we wait. Heaven, wasn't I afraid! But not she, she's as cold as a fish! At last we hear footsteps. I stand against the wall, and the old man comes in. She says, as sweet as sugar: "I fear your stomach is bothering you again, dear. I'll make the powder!" He says: "Thank you! You are always so thoughtful! My friends out there only laugh at my troubles." She looks at me over his shoulder, and nods. I think: now or never! I jump forward and stick my knife in his back. Fortunately there wasn't much blood. We take off his robe and she notices there's a sealed envelope in his sleeve. She pushes it into my hands and says: "Take that— it may be money!" I put it in my jacket. Then we place him in the clothes-box, seal the lid with plaster, and let it down into the hole. I shovel back the earth, replace the stone flags, and we push the bedstead back. As I am going to put the old man's robe on, she suddenly embraces me and says, "Take me!" I say I have work to do, what does she think, the crazy slut! I put his cap on my head. Then she says: "The moon is out, they'll recognize you!" She takes her scissors and cuts me here, under my hair. I bleed like a pig! I smear that blood over my face, and run out into the garden. When I have given the fellows in the pavilion a good look at me, I make for the river and jump in. Our house was on the bank, so I have known that river since I was a child. But I tell you that the water was cold! And with that extra robe on, I was glad when I saw a good place on the bank, with a lot of shrubs. I climb on land, make a bundle of the old man's robe, throw his cap into the water, and creep into the undergrowth to wring my clothes dry.'

He looked over his shoulder, smirking. Judge Dee knew that the misguided youngster, carried away by his tale, had now got over his fright and was actually enjoying himself. He had now reached his wretched ideal, being looked upon as a dangerous criminal. The judge had learned all he wanted, he could tell the Student to shut up and sign his confession. But he decided to let him finish. The youngster had cowardly killed a defenceless old man, but the judge was convinced that the woman had goaded him on. And there were worse crimes, much worse than an actual murder. He thought with distaste of the task ahead, after the session.

The Student took a sip of tea, spat on the floor and continued:

'Back in the inn I open that envelope. No money, no such luck! Only a book with financial notes. I think I'll show it to her, perhaps she can find out from it whether the old geezer had other cash somewhere in the house. I went to see her the next day. We open the safe, but no two hundred gold pieces! I should have understood then what she was really up to! But, fool that I am, I help her search. Nothing doing, of course! I show her the notebook, but she can't make head or tail of it. There we were! She says she'll look everywhere for the gold, it must be there. If she doesn't find it, she'll sell her trinkets, we'll go away as soon as we have the necessary cash. I think, all right, I am fed up with this town anyway, I can sell her to a brothel on the road and perhaps make a gold bar. She isn't so new any more, but she knows at least what men want! When I am back at the inn I want to throw that notebook away. Then I think, you never know, I better have a second look at it, some time. I give it to the girl there to keep for me, she's sweet on me too, you see. And the men are always snooping around in my room. Well, I think that's about all.'

Judge Dee motioned to the scribe. He rose and read aloud his notes of the Student's confession. The Student agreed that it was correct and impressed his thumb-mark at the end of each sheet. Then the headman brought the papers over to Mrs Ko. She also impressed her thumb-mark on them.

The judge said something to Magistrate Teng. He cleared his throat and spoke:

'This court finds Mrs Ko, née Hsieh, and Hsia Liang guilty of the premeditated murder of the silk merchant Ko Chih-yuan, and proposes the death sentence for them both. The higher authorities shall decide the manner of their execution, in relation to the degree of their respective guilt.'

He rapped his gavel, and Mrs Ko and the Student were led away.

XVII

A loud murmur of voices rose from the crowd. Magistrate Teng had to rap his gavel several times. A cup of tea was placed at Judge Dee's elbow. He looked round and saw Chiao Tai standing beside his chair. Apparently he had been there for some time, for his face was pale and drawn. The judge said to himself that Chiao Tai was never very lucky in his amorous escapades. He took a few sips, then said to Magistrate Teng:

'Would you have the banker Leng Chien called now, please?'

As the headman went to fetch the banker from the jail, Judge Dee pulled the notebook from his sleeve and gave it to Teng, saying: 'This is the book Hsia Liang spoke about. It gives all details about Leng's fraud, written out in his own hand.'

When Leng Chien had stated his name and profession, Judge Dee spoke:

'You stand accused of fraud, having systematically robbed your associate, the late Ko Chih-yuan, for an amount totalling one thousand gold pieces. You yourself recorded everything in your notebook here. This court shall make a careful study of all pertinent documents and establish the extent of your fraud. Now, however, you are granted the opportunity to make a concise confession.'

'I confess to having robbed my associate Ko Chih-yuan,' Leng Chien said in a tired voice. 'I am a ruined man, but I know at least that I have not driven my partner to his death! At last I can feel at peace!'

'The same goes for your creditors!' the judge said dryly.

'The other day you didn't show much concern over their interests! In due time the various creditors can submit their claims to this court for settlement.' Turning to Teng, he asked: 'Do you agree that the accused shall be remanded into custody, pending a second hearing after all pertaining documents have been studied?'

'I agree,' Teng replied. 'Leng Chien, this court finds you guilty of fraud. It shall propose a term of imprisonment for you commensurate with your crime, as soon as the investigation shall have been concluded. Lead the prisoner back to jail!'

He rapped his gavel three times and closed the session.

The two judges passed through the unicorn screen to the private office, followed by Chiao Tai and Pan Yoo-te.

Magistrate Teng said with a wan smile:

'Well, you solved all my problems for me, Dee! I'll go to my library now and change. Please have a cup of tea with me there later, when you have rested a while. Now that our journey to the Prefecture is off, we have plenty of time! We must plan a few excursions together for this week. There are some interesting places out in the mountains which I would like to show you.'

He bowed and left. Pan Yoo-te asked to be excused, as he had to go to the chancery to draw up with the scribes the official report on the court proceedings, to be forwarded to the Prefect. As Judge Dee sat down in an armchair, Chiao Tai placed a large package wrapped in coloured paper on the desk and said:

'Here is your silk, Magistrate! Very best quality, as per order. I had a look at the villa of Mrs Teng's sister. A very fine place, lots of money, I'd say. It all belongs to her, for Mrs Teng was her only sister. The servants also said that Leng Te used to stay out there regularly. He did several paintings of the garden; they are now hanging in the reception hall. Leng Te's death was a great blow to all of them out there.'

Judge Dee nodded. He pensively tugged at his moustache. After a while Chiao Tai asked:

'How did you know that the Student murdered old Ko, sir?'

The question startled Judge Dee from his musings.

'The Student, you say? Oh, there were no less than four facts that pointed at him. First, when your adventure showed how little Mrs Ko had cared for her husband, I immediately thought, of course, of her having had a lover who could have been involved in Ko's demise. As a matter of fact, the Student was due to meet Mrs Ko that night, but he couldn't keep the appointment because I took him with me to the marsh. Second, on that trip the Student boasted to me that he was going to bring off a big coup, all by himself. Later he told you that he was going to get two hundred gold pieces, and both Leng Chien and Kun-shan said there had been two hundred gold pieces in Ko's safe. Third, when Baldy struck the Student in the face on our first night at the Phoenix Inn, the youngster started to bleed profusely, and Baldy remarked that there was a previous knife wound on his forehead. It was, however, the fourth and last fact that made me suddenly see all the others in their proper connection. I mean Kun-shan's statement that he had discovered Leng Chien's water-stained notebook hidden behind the bed in Carnation's room. I had noticed that the girl was fond of the Student, and the pleading look she gave me when Kun-shan said he had found the book in her bedroom told me that the Student must have asked her to keep it for him, but that she didn't want the Corporal to know. For the Corporal is willing to share her only with Baldy and a few selected friends—apart from "outside work", of course. Heaven, that reminds me! The

172

fellow is still in jail! Tell the headman to bring him here!'

When the headman had brought the Corporal and made him kneel in front of Judge Dee's chair, the judge motioned him to leave them alone. He said to the Corporal:

'Rise, and let's have a friendly talk!'

The Corporal got up and stared dejectedly at the judge and Chiao Tai from under his ragged eyebrows. Wrinkling his low forehead, he said bitterly:

'So you are really a thief-catcher, and he is your running dog! Heaven, can a man never trust anybody?'

'If I acted a part,' Judge Dee said, 'it was only because I needed your help in solving a sordid crime. You did indeed help me, and I did enjoy your hospitality. I noticed that you maintain strict discipline among your men, you keep them to begging and other smaller offences and see to it that they commit no real crimes. I also had the military police look up your army record.'

'So it's worse than I thought!' the Corporal muttered. 'That means my head! Well, it wasn't much of a head-piece anyway!'

'Shut up and listen!' Judge Dee said impatiently. 'I have decided that you shall go back to the Imperial Army, that's where you belong. Baldy shall keep the men under control, as you taught him. Here is a letter to the garrison headquarters, stating that you did useful work for the magistrate, who proposes that you be re-enlisted and pro- moted to sergeant. Go now and take this to the officer in charge of personnel there.'

'Better to Captain Mao, he knows him!' Chiao Tai inter- rupted.

'To Captain Mao then. And when they have issued to you your helmet, cuirass and sword,' Judge Dee continued with a smile, 'you'd better dress yourself up in them and show yourself to Carnation. Keep her for yourself, Sergeant Liu, she's too fine a woman to share. And she needs you.' He took the package Chiao Tai had brought from the desk and held it out to the Corporal, saying: 'Give her this small present from me, I want her to look nice as a sergeant's wife! And tell her that I am sorry I can't call myself your "cousin"!'

The Corporal stuffed the letter into his belt, and tucked the package under his muscular arm. Then he gave the judge a dazed look. Suddenly his face lit up, and he shouted: 'Sergeant, by Heaven!' He turned round and rushed out.

'So that's why you had him arrested!' Chiao Tai said with a grin.

'You don't think he would have come to the tribunal of his own free will, do you?' Judge Dee asked. 'And I hadn't got the time to go hunting for him. We'll be leaving for home too, presently. Send a constable to the Hostel of the Flying Crane to get the clothes bundle we left there, and tell the groom here to select two good horses for us.'

The judge quickly rose and took off the damask robe and the official cap. Putting his own, well-worn black cap on his head he left the office and went across the large central courtyard to the magistrate's private residence.

XVIII

The old steward came to meet him, and led him to the library.

Magistrate Teng had changed into an informal robe. He invited the judge to sit down next to him on the broad bench, and told the steward he could go. The scene reminded Judge Dee of their first meeting there. While the magistrate was pouring out a cup for Judge Dee, he noticed that his guest looked at the empty side wall where the lacquer screen had stood. He said with a sad smile:

'I had the screen removed to the store-room. You'll understand, it reminded me too much of . . .'

Judge Dee abruptly set down his teacup. He said sharply:

'Spare me, I pray you, a repetition of that tale of the lacquer screen! Once is enough!'

Teng looked, dumbfounded, at Judge Dee's impassive face. Then he asked:

'What on earth do you mean by that remark, Dee?'

'Exactly what I said,' the judge replied coldly. 'It was a nice, sentimental tale, and you told it well. I was quite touched, the other night. But it's a fantasy from beginning to end, of course. Your late wife had only one sister, not three—to mention only one small matter.'

Magistrate Teng's face went livid. His lips moved, but no sound came forth. Judge Dee rose and walked over to the open window. His hands behind his back, he looked at the waving bamboos in the garden outside. Then, keeping his back turned to Teng, he spoke:

'Your story of the lacquer screen was as fantastic as the one about your love for your wife, Silver Lotus. You love only one person, Teng, and that is yourself. And your fame as a poet, of course. You are an extremely conceited and utterly selfish man, but you never suffered from any attacks of insanity. I suspect, however, that nature stunted you in another manner. Since you remained childless and never took other wives or concubines, you utilized your defect for building up your false reputation as the "eternal lover". I hate adulterous women, but I'll say for your wife that her life with you must have been very unhappy.'

The judge paused. He heard only the heavy breathing of the magistrate behind him.

'One day,' he resumed, 'you began to suspect that your wife had adulterous relations with the young painter Leng Te. She must have first met him at the country house of her elder sister. I assume that they were drawn to each other by the fact that both of them were living under a dark shadow—he knew that he hadn't long to live, and she was married to a cold and cruel husband. You had to be sure, so you followed them secretly to their rendezvous in the house near the west gate, and spied on them. You had covered your face with your neck-cloth, but the woman in charge there remembered your limp. Pan Yoo-te had told me that at about that time you had sprained your ankle. That temporary limp was a good disguise, for it would distract attention from your other features, yet disappear as soon as it was healed. I had forgotten all about it, but last night my assistant Chiao Tai made a remark about Kun-shan's broken ankle, and then I remembered what Pan had told me, and the truth dawned on me.

'The chastity of women is the basis and fundament of our sacred social order, and the law prescribes death for both the adulterous woman and her paramour. Having caught the pair in the act, you could have killed them then and there. Or you could have denounced them to the Prefect, and both

176

would have been decapitated. But your conceit prevented you from taking either of those courses. You couldn't bear to see the carefully built picture of the "eternal lovers" destroyed, you couldn't bear it to become known that your wife had deceived you. You decided to say nothing, but to prepare a scheme to kill your wife without it becoming known that you did so to take revenge for her infidelity, and which would confirm rather than destroy the image of the "eternal lovers"—and all that without running the risk of being prosecuted for murder, of course. Your grandfather's mental disease and the lacquer screen gave you the idea. It was a very clever idea, Teng. You must have brooded over it many an evening, sitting alone in your library here. Perhaps at the same time your wife was meeting her lover in her sister's villa, but that didn't bother you. For you didn't care a pin for her. On the contrary, I think you hated her, because she was a really great poetess, Teng, and you stole your best lines from her work. You were jealous of her talent, and therefore you prevented her from having her poetry published. But I saw her own manuscript copy, and I tell you that you'll never reach that sublime height, Teng.

'You thought out an excellent story. It had all the requirements for becoming a famous tale, told and retold in literary circles all over the Empire, with admiration and sympathy. There was an old family curse, there was a haunting antique screen, there was romance—I for one started by believing every word of it, and I was deeply moved. If all had gone according to plan, you would have killed your wife in a carefully staged fit of insanity. Then you would have denounced yourself to the Prefect, who of course would have acquitted you. You could have retired on a pension and devoted the rest of your life to building up further your fame as a poet. You have no interest in women, so you wouldn't remarry, you would mourn faithfully for your wife till the end of your days.

'I don't doubt that you had an equally ingenious plan for taking revenge on Leng Te. But he died before you could execute that scheme. You gloated over your wife's despair. I hear that the last two weeks you have been exceptionally cheerful, while your wife became ill.

'Kun-shan murdered your wife. She never knew what happened to her, and she died in peace. You entered the dressing-room just after Kun-shan had emptied the full contents of his infernal blowpipe there, and the drug overpowered you. When you came to, you thought it had been you who had killed her. That didn't particularly distress you. You then became frantic only because you assumed that too much brooding over your scheme had ended up by really affecting your brain. That priceless brain of the great poet! You were so worried about yourself that when I came unexpectedly to see you, you didn't have the presence of mind to put into operation your scheme of the lacquer screen. In your confusion you told the steward that stupid lie about your wife having gone to visit her sister, and you got rid of me as quickly as possible. However, after the session, when you had calmed down, you realized that my arrival in Wei-ping was a godsend. You now had a witness to confirm your story of the lacquer screen, a colleague who would go with you to the Prefect and whose testimony would lend even more colour to the tragedy. So you sent your headman to summon me, to hear your touching confession.

'But I couldn't be found. In the state of mind you were in, that disappointment unduly disturbed you. You began again to doubt your own sanity, and the soundness of your scheme. The servants began to wonder about the locked bedroom. The presence of the dead body there began to haunt you. Thus you took the foolish step of removing your wife's body to the marsh, without even examining it.

'Late that night I finally did come. You told your story with relish, and your confidence returned. But to your great disappointment I then began to talk about unclarified points, hinting at the possibility that you had *not* killed your wife. Nothing could have been more unwelcome to you! Then, however, you remembered that, since you had made the mistake of removing the body, I might perhaps hit on a good idea for glossing over that blunder. Therefore you consented to postpone our visit to the Prefect, and gave me a free hand to try to locate the real killer—convinced as you were that there was no such person.

'Now everything has turned out very well indeed for you. It's true that you don't have the satisfaction of having killed your wife yourself, but on the other hand now you'll be even more of a tragic hero. Your beloved wife was brutally murdered! I don't doubt that in the coming years your name as a poet will grow steadily. The tale of the lacquer screen is off, but that of the inconsolable lover will do nicely too. Your poetry won't become better, but people will say that's because of the cruel blow that shattered your happiness. Everybody will pity you and praise your work even more highly than before. I wouldn't be astonished if you became the Empire's leading poet, Teng!'

Judge Dee paused. Then he concluded in a tired voice:

'That's all I wanted to say to you, Teng. Of course I shall keep all I discovered about you a deep secret, for ever. Only don't expect that I shall ever read your poetry again!'

There was a long pause. The judge heard only the rustling of the green bamboo leaves in the garden outside. At last Magistrate Teng spoke:

'You wrong me deeply, Dee. It is not true that I didn't

love my wife. I loved her dearly. It was only the fact that offspring was denied to me that cast a shadow over my happiness. Her adultery was a cruel blow that broke my heart. In fact, it brought me to the verge of insanity. It was during those fits of brooding in the deepest despair that I evolved that horrible tale of the lacquer screen. Since, as you yourself stated just now, although I had the full right to kill my wife I didn't do so, and since Kun-shan's confession has closed the case, it was quite unnecessary and wholly superfluous for you to speak to me as you did now. Even though you knew that the story about the lacquer screen was not true, you ought to have had pity on a disillusioned man, and not have exposed all my shortcomings and weaknesses as cruelly and sneeringly as you did just now. I am deeply disappointed in you, Dee, for you were always described to me as a charitable and just man. It is not charitable to humiliate and debase me just in order to show off your own cleverness. And it is not just to vilify me, alleging that I hated my wife, justifying your completely unwarranted meddling in my private life by fantastic deductions which lack all concrete proof.'

Judge Dee turned round to face his host. Fixing him with his piercing eyes, he said coldly:

'I never accuse anyone without concrete proof. Your first visit to the house near the west gate was fully justified, for you had to verify the adultery. Had you then rushed inside and killed them both on the spot, or run off and killed yourself, or done Heaven knows what other desperate deed, I would have believed that you loved your wife, or at least would have given you the benefit of the doubt. But you went back to the house and spied on them a second time. That reveals your depraved character, and supplies all the concrete proof I need. Good-bye!'

The judge bowed and left.

He found Chiao Tai waiting for him in the courtyard of the tribunal, holding two horses by the reins.

'Are we really going back to Peng-lai, Magistrate?' he asked. 'You have been here only two days, you know!'

'Long enough,' Judge Dee said curtly. He swung himself into the saddle and they rode out into the street.

They left the city by the south gate. As they were riding along the sandy highway, the judge heard something crackle in his sleeve. Guiding his horse with his knees, he felt for it and found it was the paper folder with the last of his red visiting-cards inscribed 'Shen Mo, Commission Agent'. He tore it into small pieces. He looked for a moment at the red scraps in the hollow of his hand, then threw them away.

They fluttered for a while behind his horse, then slowly sank down together with the settling dust.

POSTSCRIPT

Judge Dee was a historical person who lived from 630 to 700 A.D. In addition to earning fame as a detector of crimes, he was also a brilliant statesman who, in the second half of his career, when he was serving as a Minister at Court, greatly influenced the internal and foreign policies of the Tang Empire. The adventures related here, however, are entirely fictitious, although many features were suggested to me by original old Chinese sources. The puzzling suicide I borrowed from a case recorded in the Chinese collection by Hsü Mu-hsi, *Ku-chin-chi-an-wei-pien* (*Strange Cases of Old and Modern Times*), published in Shanghai in 1920; it is the fourth case of the third section. Judge Dee's method of making Kun-shan confess was practised in China as early as the third century A.D. When a thief called Shih-ming stubbornly refused to confess even under severe torture, a judge of that time 'had the chains taken off the prisoner, gave him food and drink and had him take a bath, so as to bring him in a happy mood. Then Shih-ming confessed and denounced all his accomplices' (see R. H. van Gulik, 'Tang-yin-pi-shih, a thirteenth-century manual of Jurisprudence and Detection', *Sinica Leidensia*, vol. X, Leiden 1956, page 181).

Note that in Judge Dee's time the Chinese did not wear pigtails; that custom was imposed on them after 1644 A.D., when the Manchus had conquered China. Before 1644 they let their hair grow long, and did it up in a top-knot. They wore caps both inside and outside the house. Tobacco and opium were introduced into China only many centuries later.

30-xii-1961   ROBERT VAN GULIK